# A Cup of Shadows

*Devecheaux Antiques and Haunted Things*

Book One

By M.L. Bullock and A.E. Chewning

Text copyright © 2020 Monica L. Bullock

All Rights Reserved

ISBN 9798682162987

## Chapter One—Aggie

My VW Rabbit had seen better days, but I still loved it. The parentals gave it to me after my sister, Patrice, had almost run it into the ground. It was quirky and unusual, like me. Let's just say I tend to be drawn to the artistic side of things. Not many people in my family cared for art of any kind, and they did not approve of my appreciation for it. Patrice included. She excelled in all things, while I wandered through life pausing on occasion to appreciate the odd yet familiar. I mean, I am an art student. I'm supposed to be weird. Yep, art wasn't my family's thing.

Except for Catholic iconography. They go gaga over all kinds of religious art. Traditional Catholic, that would be the way to describe my family. Very devout, to say the least. Hence, my wonderful name, Mary Agnes. Yep, and with a last name of Kelly; you guessed it, I'm the girl with three first names. Needless to say, I was made fun of all my life. Maybe that's what contributed to my quirkiness. Who knows?

I sat in the car and debated whether to go into the antiques shop to apply for the position that was listed in the paper. Did I want to open this can of worms? My parents were already upset that I hadn't picked Springhill College to attend in the fall.

"It's tradition," was all I heard for weeks after my application to the University of South Alabama was accepted. Even Patrice didn't get it. "Really, Aggie? Do you have to buck Mom and Dad on everything?"

*Ah, heck. I have a habit of breaking tradition, so why stop now?*

Even my chosen major, art history, sent them into a collective frenzy—enough to want to check my psychological state of mind. You would have thought I murdered someone. They wanted me to teach. Anything. Any grade. Or go into nursing.

Gross. Yuck. Just the thought made me want to hurl.

Photography was my true passion, and I would never abandon it. I loved it. Capturing that special moment in time was pure magic. Freezing it for people to see and appreciate forever. The University of South Alabama wasn't too far from our Springhill home; that was my only saving grace in that situation.

The antiques shop's parking lot was small. I could see into the window from where I was parked. There wasn't much movement in there, just an occasional shadow that moved across the wall.

Interesting. I liked it already. My parents would not be too happy that I would be working for this particular couple. Word was that the Devecheauxs were a little different. People whispered all kinds of rumors about them. Mr. Devecheaux supposedly sidelined as a drag queen in New Orleans. His wife was tied to a missing person's case, and people even suggested she might have been involved. No one openly complained about their biracial union, but trust me, it was fodder for gossip. I didn't care. Okay, I was curious. I got out of the car and walked up the steps to Devecheaux Antiques. Yep, I liked the name too.

A soft bell clanged as I opened the old-fashioned wooden door. Antiques filled every corner of the room but tastefully so. I spotted a room beyond and could see there were even more items in the back. It smelled old and familiar. Why did antiques stores always have the same smell?

"Hello?" I called politely. I couldn't see anyone at the front of the store.

"Hello," a man's voice called faintly. "I'm back here."

"Okay. Um, I'm here to apply for the position," I called back to the disembodied voice.

"I'll be right there," the voice replied cheerfully.

I stood in anticipation of who would finally appear as a man approached me. He had a kind and welcoming smile stretched across his face. I was glad he wasn't a spirit.

"I'm Henri," he said, holding his hand out to me. "Henri Devecheaux."

"Nice to meet you, Henri. I'm Aggie. Mary Agnes Kelly." I shook his hand confidently.

"Let me grab an application for you," Henri said politely. "Quick question. Are you okay with part-time? That seems to be a sticking point for a few applicants. We can't take on full-time help at the moment," he said as he reached behind the counter and retrieved a single sheet of paper.

"Yes, that's actually better for me. I have school starting in a few weeks."

Handing the application to me, he appeared to breathe a sigh of relief. "Great! We need someone on the weekends, mostly to help clean up items that come in during the week. You'd also be doing some light research. We have a system we use for dating items and whatnot. And you might have to ring up customers if we're not here. How do you feel about that?" Henri asked as he studied me closely. "Are you okay with cleaning? That's also a sticking point for some folks."

Why would anyone mind cleaning? Seemed like an easy job. And I preferred not to work with people if at all possible. A few customers, sure, but working with antiques, cleaning them? Uh, yeah. This sounded like my dream job. I wanted it more with every passing second.

"I'm fine with cleaning, and I'm pretty flexible with my time. I could do weekends or during the week for now until I start college this fall." Was it possible that I might get this job?

"College? Where will you be attending?"

"USA. Art history is my major." I waited to hear what he thought about that.

"That's great! Fill out the application, and I'll give it to the boss. She has the last word in these things." He handed me a pen to go with the application. I immediately began scribbling out my name and contact information.

"The boss? I thought you were the boss, Mr. Devecheaux. This is your place, right?"

Henri shook his head and laughed softly. "No. I'm the boss's husband." He chuckled at his own confession. "My wife, Detra Ann, makes these decisions, but I'll put in a good word for you. Good luck, Aggie. When you're done, just leave the application on the counter. Make sure we have a number for you."

"Thanks," I answered as he disappeared into the other room. It didn't take long to fill the application out. I didn't have much in the way of work experience, but I had a keen interest in art and art history and made sure I included that information on the application. When I was done, I left the paper on the counter along with the pen. I crossed my fingers and walked out into the bright sunshine.

When I left Devecheaux Antiques, I was certain I'd get a call soon—maybe even that day—but it didn't happen. It was the only application that I did want to hear back from, but at this point, I was desperate for work. I applied for fast-food restaurant gigs and one office job that I wasn't qualified for at all. None of those seemed as appealing. I didn't want to work around food. Or people.

Handling antiques would have its potential challenges, but I'd much rather deal with my issue—as I liked to call my abilities—than sling fries all day. Smelling like greasy food 24/7 didn't sound like my cup of tea.

I checked my phone for messages and sighed. It wasn't until I got on my laptop to check my email again that I found what I was looking for. An email from Devecheaux Antiques!

The subject line read: APPLICATION. I couldn't click on it fast enough.

*Dear Miss Kelly,*

*Thank you for submitting your application. I would like to set up an interview for this week. Please respond with the best day and time.*

*Sincerely,*

*Detra Ann Devecheaux*

I immediately responded that I was available in the morning. The sooner the better. Thankfully, she emailed right back. I spent the rest of the night trying to select an appropriate outfit. I wanted to make a good impression and hopefully not come off as too "quirky." I called it an early night but didn't sleep too well. Who else besides me would be this excited about working at a dusty antiques store?

I don't know what I expected. Detra Ann was blond and beautiful. There wasn't a hair—or anything, for that matter—out of place. She was the complete opposite of me. Pretty women made me nervous. I always felt like I didn't measure up. Stupid, I know.

My idea of antiques store assistant work clothes meant I could wear my best jeans, Vans, and a Marilyn Monroe t-shirt. This appeared to be a clear misstep on my part.

Mrs. Devecheaux's tailored, brightly colored pantsuit and matching lipstick reminded me of a magazine model. Was she wearing pearls too? Dang. Total miscalculation.

"Miss Kelly, it's very nice to meet you," she said, holding her manicured hand out to me.

"Call me Aggie, please." I shook her hand and tried not to break it.

Sunlight streamed in through the front windows, filling the store with a golden light. It was lovely in here. "Have a seat. Henri tells me you're going to the University of South Alabama." We perched at the front counter on expensive-looking barstools.

"Yes, this fall."

"Art history, I see. That's great." Detra Ann jotted something down on my application. I hoped it was something good. I couldn't see without my glasses.

She continued, "Henri says that you are pretty flexible with your time?"

"Yes, ma'am. I can be here whenever you need me. Until college starts, and then I'd have to work around my school schedule. Not sure what that is yet, though."

"Great. I can live with that, and I like seeing a young person take their college career seriously. That's always a good thing. I'm a firm believer in self-improvement."

She paused again and wrote something else down. Interviews were so strange. It's one person telling another person why they would be good at something that for the most part they probably have no idea whether or not they can even do. I had very little experience cleaning antiques. I just needed a job, and this seemed like a cool place to work. These were nice people; I could feel that about them. I needed to put my cards on the table.

"I'm going to be honest with you, Mrs. Devecheaux." I couldn't believe what I was about to say.

"Please, call me Detra Ann. Do be honest, Aggie. I prefer honesty."

"Okay, Detra Ann it is. I think you have a cool shop here. I love antiques and really would love to work with y'all. The truth is, and I guess you've read it from that application, I don't have a lot of experience with anything much at all. But I am honest to a fault, and I am a quick learner."

Detra Ann put her pen down. I sat there staring back at her, my heart racing, and I swear a drop of sweat rolled down my back. Nervous was an understatement. I wasn't sure why I had just blurted that out. I surely wasn't gonna get this job now.

*Crap! What was I thinking? There's no way she's going to hire me.*

"Sorry to have wasted your time." I started to get up. "It was nice meeting you."

"Wait," Detra Ann said, "why are you leaving?"

Stunned, I sat back down. "Because most people don't like my bluntness."

"I find it refreshing," Detra Ann replied, smiling with her perfect lips. "I like an honest person, and I have a good feeling about you, Mary Agnes Kelly. Excuse me, Aggie. I have a good feeling about you. If you're willing to learn how we do things—and have a teachable attitude—I think you'd be perfect."

"You do?" I definitely questioned her reasoning.

"Yes, I do. When can you start?"

"Right n-n-n-ow," I stuttered in disbelief.

"Great! I'll get you an apron and show you what I need. This place is a mess, and we've got a Grand Opening soon. I mean, we've been open, but that was our soft opening. The big one is in just a week. You turned up in the nick of time."

I couldn't believe my ears. Finally, my honesty was paying off. This would be the perfect job as long as my "issue" did not rear its ugly head. The possibility of it happening did scare me a little. This was the perfect place for it to manifest, but Detra Ann said she had a good feeling about me. She had to know what she was talking about, right? It was a risk I'd have to take.

Eventually, I'd have to come clean. My issue wouldn't be quiet forever. But until then, I would make the most of this opportunity.

Joyfully I tied on a black apron and followed Detra Ann through the store as she pointed out different displays and explained the process of taking in both consignment and direct sale items.

Finally, Mary Agnes Kelly caught a break.

## Chapter Two—Detra Ann

"I hate this painting," I complained as I rubbed my shoulders. Why wouldn't this chill go away? I prayed I wasn't coming down with something, but with Chloe in day care three days a week, I couldn't rule that out. They were always sending notes home reminding parents not to send their children to day care with a fever. Who did that kind of thing?

"You say that every session, but you never say why. What is it about it that elicits such strong emotion from you?"

I sighed as I tossed my hair over my shoulder. "You should really take a look at the new oils we have in the shop. Anything is better than this, no offense." I didn't answer my therapist's question. I should have canceled this session. Clearly, I wasn't in the mood to be interrogated...or talk to anyone. Actually, I only made the observation because I immediately regretted making my previous confession. But I did hate the painting, and for the life of me, I couldn't say why. The colors, maybe? The odd shadows at the edge of the covered bridge? Why *did* I experience such revulsion when I stared at it too long?

"It reminds me of a scene." I shrugged as I turned away from the gilded frame and the fireplace where it hung. I sat on the couch and pulled my expensive handbag to me like it was a security blanket. "Maybe a scene from a movie? One I didn't like."

"I see," Dr. Kepler said in his smooth-as-butter voice. Seriously, the man could have made it in radio. "What kind of movie? A scary one?"

"Why? Is that important? I know antiques and paintings, and it makes sense that I would have an opinion about yours." I rubbed my hands briefly before putting them in my lap. *Why am I so cold?* "I don't remember which movie, but I don't really watch scary films."

He tapped his pen on his desk before joining me. As always, he carried his notebook with him. Dr. Kepler sat in the chair opposite me; his hazel eyes softened, but that familiar gleam of his remained. The gleam that promised more questions. He reminded me of a bloodhound that had treed a raccoon. And I was the unlucky raccoon.

"You're deflecting, Detra Ann. Let's rewind this conversation a tad. What did you mean when you said that you are a human lie detector? You can't just blurt that out and expect me not to ask you about it. I know you well enough to know that you want and need to talk about it."

Why had I opened my big mouth in the first place? I should have known Dr. Kepler wouldn't accept my confession at face value. He was a man of science who dealt in facts, figures and case studies. Not the paranormal. As if he read my mind, understood my reticence, Dr. Kepler smiled patiently. "Okay, you said you were a lie detector. My question was did you mean that literally? Could you explain that, please?"

I shivered again at the persistent chill. "Forget I said anything. Is it cold in here to you, Doctor?"

Dr. Kepler's upper lip quivered a bit. That was his tell. He was losing patience with me, but again, the bloodhound in him wouldn't let it go. "Ah, another attempt at deflection. That's twice in less than five minutes. Don't back away from this, Detra Ann. I hear you and I understand that talking about this is important to you. Let's talk about it. Don't worry about what I will think. I am not going to judge you or condemn you. I hope you trust me. After all this time, you should be able to trust me."

I nervously twisted at a loose strand of hair and tucked it behind my ear. "No one ever believes me—not at first—but my gift doesn't let me down. It's like playing the piano or writing poetry. Lie detecting is a thing I do. I don't think about it. I don't doubt it or study it. I just do it."

"Tell me how that works."

Heaven knows why I decided to tell him this today. We were coming to the end of our year-long series of therapy sessions. Maybe I was grasping at straws. Could it be that I wasn't ready to let go of Dr. Kepler? *Dang, didn't see that coming.* That could be it.

But why? I managed life and love and work just fine nowadays. I couldn't see myself climbing back into a bottle, but I guess anything was possible. I had too much to lose now. Too much to live for—I had a thousand reasons to stay sober. Detra Ann Devecheaux had everything under control!

*So why am I dragging my feet and deliberately dispersing land mines that will hinder my own progress?*

"We've been meeting for nearly a year, and I have to say this is the first time you've shared anything remotely remarkable with me. This is the fork in the road, Detra Ann. You can go left, or you can go right. It's decision time."

The chill returned, but I couldn't take my eyes off Dr. Kepler. His excitement about my confession surprised me. Was it really that big of a deal? Could he be right? Was this my pivotal moment? I'd just about given up on having one. He was right; these sessions had become pretty predictable, boring, meaningless. Then I understood that it was all me. This was what I needed to talk about. Not Henri's poor decision-making. Not my need for perfection. Not my mother's lifelong career as a social climber.

This was the thing. Well, I couldn't quit now. Dr. Kepler was right. I needed to talk about this. I'd worked too hard at trying to be normal. All this time I'd wished for the courage to take a hard look at who I truly was, and this was that moment. He was right—I could feel it.

Then it all came out. I told him about the first time and the last time I knew someone was lying to me. I explained how it made me feel when I realized I was being lied to. I was still talking when his receptionist called to remind him that his next appointment had arrived. I hadn't even given him a chance to question me.

"Okay, Amanda. Five minutes." Dr. Kepler hung up the phone and sat on his desk. His eyes were still riveted on me, but they were softer now. It was as if he were seeing me for the first time. To my surprise, he smiled. "You did good, Detra Ann. How do you feel?"

That's when I noticed that I wasn't shivering anymore. In fact, the whole room appeared to have lightened. It was as if whatever clouds had gathered inside and outside had diminished during my confession. What a strange sensation. I smiled back at Dr. Kepler.

"Honestly? Pretty good. Thanks for not laughing at me. But I have to ask…"

"No, I don't think you're crazy."

I reached for my purse and walked toward the door. "How did you know that's what I was going to ask?"

"Because that's what everyone asks. You are not crazy, but you know I'm fascinated. We'll talk more next week. In the meantime, I want you to try something. We've talked about it before and I know it's not your favorite thing, but I think it would help you."

I was genuinely puzzled. "What is it?"

"I want you to keep a journal. Starting from today until next week when we meet. Don't write about the past; write about your day."

"Okay, I guess I could do that. I have to ask, what's the purpose of this exercise?"

"I don't want you to think about that. Trust me. I'll see you next Friday. Bring your journal. Consider it homework."

"Challenge accepted, Dr. Kepler. See you Friday."

I stepped out into the sunshine feeling fifty pounds lighter.

## Chapter Three—Aggie

My first three days at the shop were fairly uneventful. I swept up and dusted, mostly. The occasional customer popped in—but that seemed to only happen in waves. I was no antiques expert, but they had some amazing things here. I hoped we sold something significant soon. I wanted to keep my job.

The back door to the shop opened, which could only mean Detra Ann had returned from her appointment and probably would check in on me. She had a habit of making sure I was doing okay, and I suspected she quietly critiqued my outfits. Thankfully, she hadn't said anything yet. I had to be me—I couldn't imagine curbing my personal style for anyone. Surprisingly, she didn't blink twice at the purple streak that ran through my light brown hair and black winged eyeliner, but the Nirvana dead smiley face t-shirt made her frown. Even my ripped, Calvin and Hobbes painted jeans were okay. Maybe my new boss had a thing against Nirvana?

Detra Ann set the box down on the counter. "Sorry I'm late. Good morning, Aggie. I've got more goodies here. Any sales this morning?"

"Good morning, Boss Lady," I said, smiling politely. "Not yet, but we've had some window-shoppers. Maybe they'll come back."

"You know I don't like that," she replied with a grin. "It's Detra Ann. Not Boss Lady."

"Sorry, Detra Ann. What do you have in the box?"

Her smile faded as she opened the dusty box. "Treasures from a friend who passed away." Detra Ann's eyes brimmed with tears and her shoulders slumped a little, and I thought she was about to break into sobs. She had not been her usual cheerful self when she arrived, but I'd never have pegged her for a crier. I prepared myself for an awkward moment; I never knew what to do.

How would I comfort a woman I barely knew? Well, I had to say something. I didn't want to leave her hanging.

"Can I do anything? Are you okay?"

My comment interrupted whatever tearful thoughts she'd been shuffling around in that blond head of hers. "I need you to clean these up for the appraiser, Aggie. I thought I could do it, but I was wrong. Mr. Ladner should be stopping by later this afternoon. Hopefully." She sniffed away the tears and turned her attention to a stack of receipts I'd left for her on the counter. *Okay. We're changing the subject. Phew.*

"Okay, will do."

I breathed a quiet sigh of relief. I was happy she didn't break down. Emotions are not something I'm good at managing, especially not someone else's. I grabbed the box from the counter and headed to the back of the store, while Detra Ann dealt with a surprise customer. There wasn't much in the box, just one set of china cups and saucers. They had an interesting floral design and looked very old and delicate. So petite and clearly vintage. They were dusty and needed some TLC.

Putting them on the table in the workroom, I counted six cups and saucers and wrote that down in the inventory list. I took measurements and wrote a description on the notepad, then entered all the information in the computer.

*Soft yellow teacups with pink and green flowers with gold edges. Matching soft yellow saucers.*

I picked up one cup to admire the gold trim and delicate floral motif. Whoever owned these had wonderful taste. Flowers weren't my thing, of course, but these were pretty. I noticed a small chip on one of the cups; it was the only imperfection I could see. I liked this set. Strangely so.

*Shoot. Why do I feel so sad?*

"Aggie," Detra Ann called from the front of the shop, "can you come up here for a minute?"

Speaking of perfect.... "Yes, of course," I called back sweetly.

"Quickly, please?" she called in her kind yet firm voice.

"Yes, I'm coming," I replied. *Geez, impatient much?* My boss had a way of being bossy without seeming like she was being bossy. I guess you could call it passive-aggressive bossiness. Detra Ann was polite to a fault. She didn't have to say she meant business; you could just tell. Her whole attitude let you know that she was in charge and she wanted things done her way. In that regard, she reminded me of my mother.

It must be a Southern lady thing. I hoped I didn't inherit the trait. I wished Detra Ann would make up her mind. Should I be cleaning antiques or working as a front shop assistant? It's not that I minded either one of those things, but I was very task-oriented. I excelled at projects when I could stay on task. What could she possibly need me for? We weren't that busy, were we?

Wow. We *were* busy. Three people were waiting in line. Detra Ann rang up the customers while I carefully packed their items so they could leave the store without breaking anything.

Twenty minutes later, I settled back into cleaning the cups. Yes, they were pretty things. These should go fast, if the appraiser didn't want to scoop them up. I had to admit, I didn't like Mr. Ladner too much. He seemed to be a little shady, if you ask me, but no one did. Mr. Ladner put off an icky vibe, and his phony persona was totally snotty.

With my glasses perched on my nose, I studied the intricate details of the gold trim and tiny flowers. The petals were painted on and had little flecks of gold that shimmered in the light. I held the cup up to look at the bottom stamp. They were so delicate that you could almost see right through them. I didn't know much about fine china, but my guess was that had to be a good thing.

*Okay, follow standard operating procedure, Aggie. Take photos. You will need them for Facebook and the website.*

The stamp on the bottom read: "Allertons, England," and it was topped with a little crown symbol.

How cute, I thought. *I wonder if the Queen of England drinks from the same type of cup?* I could just picture her sitting there with her tea and scones. I arranged the cups on a soft cloth so I could take those photos. *Wait a second.* I counted the set again, and there were only five cups and saucers. *Um, no.* There had been six for sure.

I went back and checked the inventory list. Yep. I definitely wrote down six sets before I was interrupted by the boss.

Now there were only five. Great. I checked inside the box again, but there was nothing to see except some wadded-up newspaper. All the sets were sitting on the counter where I had counted them except one, the chipped one.

Maybe Henri came in and moved it? Why would he move just one set, though?

I continued to search, looking in the front of the store where Detra Ann had been sitting. Nope. No cup or saucer to be found. How could a cup and saucer just disappear?

*That's it. I'm going to be fired from my first job in my first week.*

## Chapter Four—Detra Ann

"We could offset costs by renting out the apartment. I agree with you, we're in a bit of a lull, but it is summer. People are at the beach or on the road traveling to more exotic locations than Mobile, Alabama. Maybe we could try a six-month lease? If we were careful and vetted the applicants, I'm sure we could find someone safe and reliable."

Henri was being remarkably patient with me, but this was an old idea—one that I didn't like at all. The idea of strangers having access to our old apartment didn't sit well with me, not to mention we'd taken to using a bit of that space as a storage area. Maybe I was panicking a bit.

In my defense, Henri wasn't good with numbers and in his mind we were going to always come out on top. Okay, maybe that wasn't fair. Henri Devecheaux knew his way around the accounting ledger, but he had some issues in the past. Major issues. He'd made some mistakes, but I wasn't going to dwell on that right now. That was all behind us.

As I tossed around ideas on how to counter his proposal, I saw a black shadow skitter across the floor on the other side of the large display table. "What in the world? Who let that cat in here?" It had to be a cat, a black cat. It wasn't large enough to be anything else.

*Oh, great. Having a cat in here would be a disaster with all these expensive, irreplaceable breakables.*

My husband gave me a quizzical look but joined me in the hunt for the unwanted feline. After five minutes of exhaustive searching and finding nothing, I gave up and shrugged my shoulders.

"Must have been a trick of the light, Harry. Sorry."

He kissed my cheek and squeezed my hand. "It's stress, sweetheart. That's all. Between your mother being sick and our daughter's wacky sleep schedule and the current sales slump, it's not hard to imagine why you'd be seeing shadows." Yeah, I must have been imagining things. "Take a day off. Go to the spa. Treat yourself, Detra Ann. While we can afford it. I'll call Aggie and see if she'll come in early. But I don't think I should miss this estate sale. I just got off the phone with Bryce. It's true. Those items from the convent are up for sale, and I think one of us should go."

I groaned inwardly. *Great. Here we are in a sales slump, and I'm letting Henri loose with the checkbook. Not smart, Detra Ann. Not smart at all.* Something in my eyes must have relayed my concern because Henri's expression shifted; he shot me those hurt puppy dog eyes. I wanted to smack him and hug him all at the same time. I didn't wait for an argument.

"No, don't do that. I'm good. Better get going, Harry. I'm rather surprised to see you so excited about nun artifacts. I'm going to look around for that cup and saucer again. I can't imagine what might've happened to it. Mary Agnes doesn't seem like the kind of person to have sticky fingers; nor does she seem like the kind to break something and not fess up. I'm sure she just misplaced it." I glanced around the room again, hoping the shadowy figure did not make a reappearance.

"I agree. I checked all the open boxes and didn't find either item. Nothing in the trash can either. If Aggie broke it, she would have dropped it in there. First-day jitters; obviously, she misplaced it. It will turn up. I have no doubt about that. Later, sweetheart. Going to find us some new treasures."

"Later!" I waved at him as he left the store and the bell on the door jangled cheerfully to announce his departure. "Please don't spend a fortune." I knew he wouldn't hear that last part, and I was okay with that. I just wanted to put it out there. *Trust him, Detra Ann. You two have been through so much together already. Surely he deserves your trust.* I sighed at my inner turmoil.

Time to think about something other than where this cup and saucer might've ended up. I glanced at the window and didn't see any passersby. This seemed like the perfect time to check out the back room where Aggie had been working yesterday. Sure, it was a little cluttered, but it was an organized mess and I knew where everything was located.

Usually.

Henri and I had walked through here twice already, and we came up empty-handed. Strange. I couldn't sell an incomplete set. I mean, I guess I could, but I knew for a fact there had been six matching cups and saucers. This was all too ridiculous.

For the next thirty minutes, I continued my search and turned up nothing. At least the remaining cups were perfect. I would hold off on listing them for now. Aggie was scheduled to come in later. Together, we could solve this puzzle. Until then, I had emails to respond to and merchandise to arrange. My business's success didn't rest upon a missing teacup. I had a beautiful Victorian jewelry collection and a miniature carousel horse that I could probably sell with a little footwork and a few phone calls. Both items had drawn a lot of interest but so far no buyers.

Yep, time to turn on the charm.

The first call I made was to Louise Hastings. I was surprised she hadn't already snagged up this collection, but then again, Louise hadn't been in the best of health lately. I dialed her number confidently and remembered to put a smile on my face. You could hear smiles over the phone. I would never have believed that except I'd seen it in action. To be honest, that was the most valuable information I took home from my business management course at Springhill College. I could almost hear Stephanie Taylor's voice in my head: "Smile before you dial." What a wise woman. I'd learned so much from her.

"Good morning, Mrs. Hastings. This is Detra Ann from Devecheaux Antiques. I'm just calling to remind you about the Victorian jewelry collection, the new one with the onyx pieces. Would you like me to send you some photographs? Perhaps book you some time in the shop alone?" She liked to do that from time to time. I didn't mind. She was a great customer, and I wanted to keep her happy.

"I'm afraid that will have to wait. My Robert is getting married again, and I'm going to be gone for the next few weeks. Perhaps when I get back, but until then, I'm holding off on doing any business. I'm sure you understand. I'm surprised your mother didn't tell you about it. How is she?"

"She's fine," I said, maintaining my smile, only this time I looked like the Joker. My pale face stared back at me in the mirror behind the register. "We haven't had much of a chance to catch up lately. Life's been so busy with our Chloe. I wish you safe travels, Mrs. Hastings. Bon voyage!" The strange thing about this relationship was that Robert wasn't Mrs. Hastings' son but rather her ex-husband. He had been married a number of times since their divorce, but he was—by all accounts—reluctant to let go of the older woman.

Yep. It was too weird.

"Well, I'm off to Europe. I'll call you when I return. Thank you, dear." And with that, she hung up.

Just in time too because a shopper entered the store. I allowed him to browse around for a few minutes and then offered to help him locate items he might be searching for.

"No, thank you. Just looking."

"Let me know if I can help you." I went back to the register and pretended to be busy but kept my eyes on the visitor. It was a shame to think about it, but there were a lot of criminals visiting our downtown area. Anything small enough to put in a coat was fair game. I hated thinking like this, but that was the truth. He left with a cheerful wave and didn't steal anything—as far as I could tell. As he walked out, two more people came in and then business picked up.

Happily, I made a few sales. When I finally got a break, I decided to pull out the laptop and take a peek at the nanny cam. Henri believed I was being intrusive, but I didn't agree. We were talking about the safety of my daughter—our daughter.

My best friend, Carrie Jo, accused me of being a helicopter mom, but she really had no room to talk. When AJ was little, she was just as bad. Granted, she'd grown out of it, but I didn't think I ever would. The world was a rotten place.

Out of the corner of my eye, I again saw a strange movement that looked like a shadow, low to the ground and cat-shaped. And I wasn't the only one who saw it. One of the customers in my shop had a toddler on her hip, and the child's eyes followed the shadow too. When she caught me looking, the child stuck her thumb in her mouth and turned to face the other way. I wanted nothing more than to follow the shadow into the other room, but the man was leading his wife to the counter.

Shoot!

They'd fallen in love with a few old books, he said. Copies of a Mark Twain collection and some other hard-to-find hardbacks. They made their purchase, and I wrapped the books in paper before putting them carefully in a bag.

"Do you like cats?" I asked the little girl, who watched me with a sullen expression. Clearly, it was almost naptime in her world. She didn't answer, but her mother smiled.

"She's obsessed with animals. All animals. Why? Is there a cat here?"

How to answer that question? "My daughter is a little younger than yours, and she is nuts for cats. We don't have an official cat here, but I'm thinking of getting one. What do you think?" I tried again to get the child to engage with me.

"Alexis, don't be rude. The nice lady is talking to you."

"I want to go home." The child turned her face away from me again, and my heart sank a little. Gee whiz. Kids were rarely crazy about me, but they didn't normally act so standoffish when I spoke to them.

Alexis' mother said, "I'm sorry. We're working on her social skills. Thank you for the books. Have a nice day." The couple and their sleepy daughter left the shop, and I immediately walked into the other room.

"Here, kitty-kitty. Kitty?" I said as I checked under the tables. It was very possible that a cat had snuck in while customers were entering or exiting the shop, but I hadn't seen one. I decided to hotfoot it out the back door to make sure there wasn't a colony of feral cats hanging around the back of the shop. It wasn't unheard of down here. Mobile really needed to do a better job of taking care of these wild animals. I tapped on the alarm pad and pushed open the back door.

Nope. Nothing to see here. Not a single cat in sight. Thankfully, there were no food cans or anything that would lure a feline to this area. Bewildered, I went back inside and tapped on the keypad again to alarm the back door. The jingling of the front door didn't give me much time to consider what I'd seen—not once but twice today.

Shoot. I almost forgot to watch the nanny cam and call the house. Chloe would be going down for her nap soon, and I liked to make the call before she got too cranky. I picked up the phone and called as I tapped on the computer screen. I didn't normally leave my laptop out—that would be the first thing to go if I wasn't careful—but I had to make sure my fussy child was behaving.

"Hi, Sharon. It's me. How's Chloe doing this morning?" The screen connected with the nanny cam. "Oh, dear. I see she's up to her elbows in Cheerios."

Sharon waved at me from the kitchen table and tried to get Chloe to wave too, but my daughter was being a fusspot just like Alexis. "Say hi to Mommy!"

"Mommy!" Chloe shouted as she tossed down her bowl and cocked her head to listen for the front door. I had to stop doing this. Henri was right; Chloe didn't understand that I wasn't home when I called. I was making things worse for Sharon, for me and most of all for Chloe.

"Sorry, Sharon. Just checking in. Will you make sure she tries to potty before she lies down? We had some success this weekend, but she's stubborn. I think it runs in my family."

The good-natured young woman chuckled while Chloe shrieked to high heaven. Dear Lord, I wasn't paying her enough.

"It's no problem. Yes, we'll try. Don't forget I have practice this afternoon. You'll be here by three, right?"

"Yes, I'll be there." We chatted a few more minutes, and I hung up the phone.

I glanced at the clock. I had a few more hours to kill before Aggie clocked in. Maybe I should rearrange the antique dice collection?

My ears began tingling, like invisible fingers were touching them.

That's when I heard the soft, pretty singing of a woman. I closed my laptop and slid it back under the counter. I glanced around the store, but there wasn't a soul in the place. Not a single soul. But I know what I heard. Only a few notes but definitely singing. A haunting tune, too.

And it was coming from upstairs.

## Chapter Five—Aggie

*Epic, Aggie. Just epic. You need this job. You need financial freedom from the parentals. You are not asking them for money. They have it and they give it to you, but that's beside the point.*

Where the heck could that cup have gone? *Okay, think Aggie, think. Step by step now.* Detra Ann was waiting for an answer. I needed to give her one. Let's see. I placed the items one by one on the table. Wrote down the numbers on the inventory sheet. Boss Lady called me. I came back, and the cup was gone. Sounds about right.

*Ugh, my life!*

Panic was setting in, and I broke out into a cold sweat. I had no answers at all. Detra Ann was going to kill me. Thank goodness the doorbell rang. Saved by a customer—for the moment.

I knew what I had to do, but I really didn't want to do it. It was tough enough going through life with my issue, and I didn't want to bring it into work. My employers would probably be weirded out, like most people, and I just didn't need that right now. But I needed this job.

*The rock and hard place—that's where I'm at. Either I'm going to lose my job because they think I'm a thief or I use my "crazy" to keep my job.* I mean, what if they thought I stole it? There was no other choice. I had to see if it worked.

No time like the present. I picked up one of the other cups. I held it in my hand and took a deep breath. I closed my eyes and waited for the image to appear. I knew it would, but time wasn't on my side.

"Aggie!" Detra Ann's voice broke my concentration. What did she want now? Probably answers. I ran up front, expecting the worst.

"Did you find it? The appraiser should be here later."

My stomach flipped, and I thought I would hurl all over her, all over the store and all over myself. "Not yet," I replied. *That's it, I'm fired.* "Still looking. Working on it. I know I'll find it, Detra Ann."

She didn't look so sure, but I managed to smile confidently. "Alright, but when you get done, we need to dust this place."

I hurried back and put the cup in my hand again. The scent of French toast hit me, sweet and syrupy with a hint of pecan. *That's strange. And yummy.*

Closing my eyes, I saw a flash of a face with white, bouncy curls framing it. A woman with a gentle smile staring back at me. Her mouth was moving, but I couldn't make out what she was saying.

*Can you speak louder? I can't hear you.*

I concentrated harder on her mouth; she was definitely saying something. It appeared to be only two words, but I still couldn't make them out. She looked sad and frustrated with me now but still gentle and serene.

Such a lovely lady, warm and inviting. You could feel her sweetness. She must have used the china at one point in time. I was pretty sure the items must be hers, but sometimes these objects that I touch lead me in different directions. Especially if they were something like this, something that could have been used by multiple people.

There was no guarantee that they were hers.

*Can you tell me your name? Do you know where the cup went? Did you take it?* The only thing I got back from her was her endearing smile. *Thanks, lady. You're sweet but no help at all.*

Well, I could run out of the store and never look back. *Aggie, put on your big-girl panties and do this.* My pep talk wasn't working. I felt dizzy as I approached the front counter.

Detra Ann was with another customer, thank goodness. Man, this was the busiest I'd ever seen this place. I pretended like I was cleaning while I waited for my execution. She had to know. I could feel it in my bones. Once she made the sale, I took my opening. The moment of truth had come. "Detra Ann, got a sec?" I reluctantly blurted out as the customer closed the door.

"Sure, Aggie. What is it?"

"Well, um, um..."

She interrupted, "You lost the cup, right?"

"I'm not sure. I know I set all of them on the table. I counted them and then came up front to assist you. When I went back, it was gone."

I waited for "you're fired" to escape her mouth, but there was no response. Nothing. She just looked at me.

"I'll leave now."

"Why?" she asked.

Geesh, why were there tears in my eyes? "I'm fired, right? I mean, why would you believe me?"

Detra Ann chuckled. "I know when people are lying to me. You aren't." I had no idea what that meant, but I was relieved.

"You believe me? I'm not fired?"

She tossed her pretty blond ponytail over her shoulder. "No, of course not. Now, let's find that cup before the appraiser gets here. It's got to be around here somewhere."

"That's the thing, I looked everywhere. It's nowhere to be found," I confessed sadly.

"Come on, Aggie. It has to be here somewhere. It couldn't have sprung legs and walked off."

"Agreed, but it's not here." She looked as perplexed as I felt. We walked to the back of the shop to pick up the search again. After a few minutes, I sighed deeply. There was no sign of the chipped cup or the saucer.

"Where did you see it last?" Detra Ann asked.

"It was right here," I said as I pointed down at the table, picking up one of the cups. "With all the others. I took it out of the box and set it right here." The sugary-sweet smell of syrup hit me again.

"Did Henri come in?" she asked as she sniffed too. Her question didn't register. I was overcome with the smell. It filled the air with its sweetness.

"Do you smell that?" I asked, taking a sniff into the air and walking back and forth. I felt like a bloodhound trying to pick up on a scent. The smell was so overpowering that I didn't care if she thought I was crazy. "The smell of pancakes or maybe French toast. You don't smell syrup?"

Detra Ann stopped moving. She froze, watching me as I searched for the mystery scent. Between the missing cup and the scent that was coming from nowhere, I felt like I was going insane. I felt off, and maybe this was just the thing to send me over the edge. I had always been different. This store seemed to be bringing out all my little idiosyncrasies.

"You smell French toast?" Detra Ann asked cautiously.

"Yes. You don't smell it?"

"No, but I believe you. Stop sniffing for a minute." Her words broke my bloodhound concentration. "I think I know why you might be smelling that scent," she calmly said.

"Really? You believe me? That's a first. People don't usually believe me." I was shocked at her calm demeanor and wondered why she hadn't kicked me out of the store and called 9-1-1.

"This china set belonged to a dear friend of mine—her name was Bette. Her son gave these to me to be appraised and then sold. They are on consignment, so losing a cup isn't great, but these things happen. I hated the thought of selling any of them, but Cleveland Hollingsworth is pretty determined to offload everything that belongs to his mother. I hate that." Detra Ann appeared solemn. It was a pained look, grief-stricken and distraught. Her eyes glistened from the tears.

I knew then that I had connected with Bette when I held the cup. No wonder she came through to me. I wish I knew what she was trying to tell me. "She's such a sweet lady," I blurted out absently.

"What?"

I still wasn't thinking about what was happening. "I mean, she seemed sweet, and all those curls. What a beautiful soul. I just wish...." I caught myself mid-sentence—and just in time from the look on Detra Ann's face. All the blood rushed out of it. Yep. I said too much.

"Did you see Bette? Here in the store?"

I wasn't sure how to back out of this one.

"Kind of. I mean, that's a guess because I've never met her. But, yes." I shrugged my shoulders and braced for more questions. I hated telling people about my visions, but in for a penny, in for a pound. Taking a deep breath, I added, "I can *see* people if they have an attachment to an object. I have to touch the object. It's called psychometry." I just blurted it out, like ripping off a bandage. Wow, that felt better than I expected.

Even if she did believe in psychic abilities, would she want someone like me in her antiques shop? I mean, that seemed like a liability for someone working around antiques. I'd probably have something happen every time I went to clean something. There was no readable expression on her face.

It felt like an eternity before Detra Ann responded, "You're telling me that you can *see* dead people?" The question lingered there before I could gather enough courage to respond.

"Yes."

This day couldn't end quick enough. Who in their right mind would want to keep me as an employee after all this? A smile spread across Detra Ann's face. "You are in good company, Aggie," she said, grabbing one of the cups off the table. "I wasn't joking when I said I was a human lie detector. It's a thing I've always been able to do. I know you're telling the truth. I can feel it, know it."

"That's amazing and also terrifying. How do you deal with being different? I've never met anyone remotely like me, and I've visited tons of so-called psychics and mediums, but nobody gets it. You mean you're okay with me being different?"

"Yes, as long as things don't disappear all the time," she joked with a rueful smile. "We'll go broke if the antiques turn up missing on a regular basis. I'll make the call to Cleveland and buy us some time. We need to find it. I have a friend who might be able to help us. She's different too. She dreams about places and people."

"What?! You're blowing my mind, Boss Lady." I sat down in the squeaky work chair and tried to process all of this. "But you know what, this cup went missing on my watch, and I'd like to try to recover it. It's obvious that Bette wants to tell us something about that cup. Let me try again. Please? I'm not really proficient, but I'd like to give it a shot."

Detra Ann walked to the open archway between the two rooms. There was no one in the shop. She picked up one of the teacups from the set and handed it to me. The cup and saucer clanked in my shaking hands.

What if I couldn't pick up anything?

I steadied my hands and closed my eyes. The smell of tea lingered in the air around me. It was different from what I smelled before. Not sweet but a light floral scent. *This friend of Detra Ann's sure likes to mix things up. Now she smells like tea. A rare, exotic tea.* I'd only smelled it a few times before. Had a bit of clove in it. Maybe.

There was a slight flash as I closed my eyes tighter.

Then the vision became clear. I could see two women, one I recognized as Bette. Her hair wasn't white in this vision but blond. However, there was no mistaking her face. The other young woman had dark hair, and her face was kind of hidden. They were sitting across from each other in a dimly lit room. No, neither one was the sweet, smiling white-haired lady I had seen before.

The blonde nervously glanced around the room as she waited for the other woman to speak. Ugh. I could feel her anxiety, and it was huge. Making me sick. This was a new experience for me. I usually saw things, not felt them.

Yeah, the blond woman felt as if her very future hung in the balance. The dark-haired lady peered intently into the cup she was holding tightly. She moved her hand slightly, and I couldn't believe my eyes.

*I know that cup!*

Clasped in the dark-haired woman's hands was the same cup that I lost. At least it was from the same set. Her dark eyes peered into the murky depths of the cup. Was she reading tea leaves?

She raised her eyes to the woman across from her, and I felt myself begin to fall deeper into the vision. For some reason, I thought of Alice, from my favorite childhood book.

*Curiouser and curiouser...*

## Chapter Six—Bette

A light tapping on the window drew my attention away from my Teen Hearts magazine. The light blue curtains in my bedroom were thin enough to reveal that I indeed had an unexpected visitor hanging outside the window. I froze on the bed. What if this was some sort of Peeping Tom? Without moving a muscle, I glanced at the pink rotary phone on the nightstand beside the bed. My thoughts were jumbled, and my pulse raced. Should I call the police or my neighbor, Mr. Jarvis? Maybe I should call my mother?

The tapping continued, and then I heard a soft voice. A young woman's voice. "Bette? Are you there?" This voice wasn't familiar, but it did not frighten me. This was no Peeping Tom. I waited another few seconds and held off reaching for the phone.

Finally gathering my courage, I asked in a firm voice, "Who's there?"

"Rosalie. From school."

"School?"

I tossed the magazine to the side and crept to the window. Sure enough, it was a familiar face; a girl I'd spoken to only in passing. The near stranger tapped on my window again. "I need to talk to you?" This unexpected visit concerned me. What could she possibly want with me?

I pulled the curtains back and lifted the window a few inches. "What are you doing tapping on my window?" Fat raindrops began splatting on the back patio below. The strange dark-haired girl would get soaked standing out there. These sudden late-summer storms could be dangerous. Lightning flashed in the distance. Yes, this would be a soaker. A frog strangler, as Mr. Jarvis called storms like these.

"I didn't want your mother to see me. I need to speak with you. May I come in?"

"We're speaking now," I answered suspiciously. "Most people use the door when they come to someone's house."

Rosalie wiped at the rain that splashed her pale face. The girl had black eyes, the darkest I'd ever seen. I'd always thought of her as exotic-looking with her luminous skin and raven-colored hair. Lovely, really, if she were to put some effort into her appearance. She dressed like a gypsy in her colorful skirts and peasant blouses, and not in a stylish manner. Her clothing always appeared too big for her, as did her sandals. Many of our schoolmates made fun of Rosalie behind her back, and sometimes to her face. I'd even heard one girl call her a witch.

Rosalie offered no excuses for coming to my window instead of the door. The rain continued to fall. It wasn't mere splotches of water but rather sheets of rain that had descended upon her. How had she gotten into the backyard? I must have left the gate unlocked again. I had a nasty habit of doing that. How many times had Mother reminded me to keep everything locked up tight? Now here I was with a stranger standing outside my window. A sad-faced, soaked stranger.

"Go to the back door, Rosalie. You will drown if you stay out there."

"Is your mother home?" she asked again.

"No. Go to the back door. It's just around the hedge here." I pointed to the right and closed my window and pulled my curtains.

Odd. How very odd.

I slid my slippers on and padded to the back door, pondering why on earth Rosalie would appear at my window. And why was she so concerned with my mother? Granted, Letitia Hollingsworth tended to suck up the air in any room she walked into. Perhaps Rosalie felt intimidated, or maybe Mother had been unkind to her in the past. It was entirely possible. I was about to find out.

With a catch of my breath, I unlocked the door. I prayed that this was not a huge mistake. I'd barely opened the door to her when Rosalie slipped inside. The slightly smaller girl dripped on the carpet runner. The rain fell quite heavily, and the house shook at the sound of thunder. I closed the door and locked it, then instructed her to wait while I fetched her a towel.

"Here you go," I called as I raced back from the downstairs bathroom, but Rosalie was not where I left her. She'd wandered into the library, Father's library, a room no one used much. "You're going to soak the carpet. Please take this and dry off." I handed her the towel and watched as she patted herself absently. Her eyes wandered around the stately room, and I could see she was clearly overwhelmed by the immense book collection and all the other treasures kept here.

"I haven't seen you at school for a while, Rosalie. I thought you moved."

Rosalie tilted her head slightly and patted her hair with the towel. The dampness of her hair and clothing lent her an otherworldly appearance. She handed me the towel with a sad smile and touched the large floor globe. She spun it gently with her fingers, something I used to do when I was a child and missed my father. Or missed the idea of him.

"My mother died. School seems pointless. Nobody likes me."

"Oh, I am sorry to hear about your mother. How awful! What about your father? Surely he expects you to finish school? To be honest, I don't think many of us like school. But it's our senior year. You'll graduate this spring with the rest of us, won't you?"

I accepted the damp towel from her pale hand and did my best to ignore the odd tingling up my spine.

"I won't graduate because I am not going back. I think I'll travel a bit."

"With your father?"

The house shook under the powerful thunder that boomed above us. "My father died a very long time ago. I do not remember him, but I wish I did. What about you? Do you remember your father?"

"How did you know my father was dead?" I tossed the towel on the wooden ladder near the bookshelf.

Her face went white, giving her a bloodless look. "I guessed. It's very dusty in here. I suppose if he were alive, he would keep it less messy," Rosalie mused as she touched the books and then paused to observe me.

"It's not that dusty, but I don't think we should stay here. It's not a room that I visit much, and I don't think my mother would like us touching his things. She's very protective of his treasures."

"I am sure she is," Rosalie said quietly. What could she mean by that?

"Let's go to the kitchen. I'll put a kettle on for some tea. You must be freezing. You must tell me why you came by, Rosalie." We walked down the black and white checkerboard hallway into the yellow kitchen. She offered no information but sat at the table and watched me fill the teapot.

"So much yellow," she commented as I set the table with teacups and saucers.

"It is Mother's favorite color. Do you like Earl Grey?"

"Yes, thank you."

*A Cup of Shadows*

I knew what she must be thinking because I thought so too. Canary yellow curtains, cream-colored cabinets. Too much yellow, and it didn't make the room any brighter. Try as I might, I never cared for the kitchen. It didn't put off a happy vibe, not at all. All the yellow in the world wouldn't change the atmosphere in here.

I sat at the table across from Rosalie. "Why did you come?"

"I'm not sure, to be honest. Where is your mother?"

Her continual questioning about my mother annoyed me, but I kept my composure. I guess I was lonelier than I imagined. I hated coming home after school to this big empty house. Mother spent much of her time traveling for business. Not that we enjoyed mother-daughter time. We didn't have that anymore. It was like she was mad at me for becoming a young woman. For growing up. I couldn't understand it.

"She's at a convention. My mother fancies herself a businesswoman. She sells makeup for a big company. Pink Flower is the name of it. Maybe you've heard of it?"

She shook her head as the tea kettle began to whistle. "Your house is grand. Do you have servants?"

I laughed at her question, not to be mean but because it seemed a funny thing to ask. "No servants. We have a housekeeper. She comes three times a week. But that's it."

"It is very grand. I like it."

"It was my father's house and his father's before him and so on. Once upon a time, they used to call it Haverty Place."

"But your last name is Hollingsworth, right?"

"It's a long story. So, tell me why you decided to bang on my window." As I began to pour the hot water into our teacups, a loud pop echoed above us and the lights went out. It was nearly pitch black in the kitchen. Wow, this storm packed a punch. "Hold on. I've got candles." I carefully made my way to the kitchen drawer and felt around for a candle, a holder and a box of matches. After a few attempts, I got the candle lit and carefully returned to the table with it. It cast the pale Rosalie in a strange glow.

"Sounds as if this storm might stick around for a bit," I said as I winced at the lightning.

"Don't worry. The lightning won't come in here." She touched my wrist briefly as if she were comforting a young child.

"I know that, but I don't like storms. Never have."

"I love them. Shall I pour the tea?" she asked in her quiet voice.

"If you like."

Rosalie poured the water into the cups, and we quietly prepared our tea.

Thunder continued to crack over the house, so loudly that the cups shook once. "It is a strong one, isn't it? I know that I owe you an explanation, but I don't know where to begin. I'm leaving soon—leaving Mobile—and I couldn't do that without telling you what I know. Even though I'm not sure you will believe me."

I stirred my tea with a dainty gold spoon. "Whatever do you mean? Is it about my mother?"

"In a way." She sank in her chair and stared into her cup. I could see that she was struggling with this confession. Or whatever it was. I didn't know how to encourage her to talk, so I just waited. I sipped my tea and watched the candle's flame dance.

"Let me read your tea leaves, Bette. I am very good at it. My mother taught me. You would have liked my mother, I think. She had a sweet soul. Her name was Camellia. Isn't that a lovely name?"

"Yes, very lovely."

She licked her lips quickly and asked in a low voice, "Have you ever heard that name, Bette?"

"I know the flowers, but I don't know anyone by that name. Why? Should I?"

She sipped her tea with downcast eyes. "I don't know. I was just curious and thought maybe your mother would have mentioned it."

The candle flickered between us. *It's my breath. I'm sure of it. That must be why it's flickering.* There were no drafts, no open windows, but the candle's flame jumped and bounced like a living thing.

"This is all so odd. Not that you're odd, but coming to my window and then the storm and now the lights. Whatever you have to say…"

The brightest flash of lightning I had ever seen illuminated the tacky yellow kitchen, but Rosalie's words were even more shocking.

"We're sisters, Bette. You and I are sisters. She never told you that, did she?"

And then the candle went out and darkness descended again.

## Chapter Seven—Aggie

I couldn't shake the vision of the two young women with the teacup even after I left the shop. Curiosity had gotten the better of me, and I couldn't help but borrow a cup and saucer from the set. I'd give it back, of course, but I just needed answers. Why did the cup go missing in the first place, and who was the dark-haired lady with Bette? I'm sure Detra Ann needed answers too. Hopefully she wouldn't be too upset with me for taking these out of the shop.

Closing the door to my room, I placed the cup and saucer down on my vanity. I wondered what Bette was so anxious about in my vision. Something was off in her life at that moment, but I just didn't know what could make that sweet woman feel that way. Before I could even get in the mindset to start with the cup, my door flung open. It was my lovely sister, the angel herself, Patrice.

"Why are you just sitting there?" she asked suspiciously.

"I'm resting," I replied tartly. "And the door was closed, Patrice. Don't you pay attention to closed doors anymore?"

"Sure, but we're sisters, Aggie. Since when do we lock each other out? Are you feeling okay? You do look kinda tired," she announced as she plopped on the corner of my bed.

Patrice had a way of knowing when I was shoveling BS her way. This was one of those moments.

"I just got home from work, and I'm tired. What do you need, Patrice?" I asked, annoyed at her interrogation.

She tossed a strand of long hair behind her shoulders. "I guess piddling around at that little antiques shop would make one tired." Boy, she had a way of making me feel an inch tall. How did she do that?

"It is harder than you think. There's lots to do around there for the Devecheauxs. Cataloging, listing, cleaning, arranging displays, dealing with customers. The whole shebang. Again, is there something I can help you with."

"I'm sure," Patrice said with a smile as she glanced at the cup set on my nightstand. "Spoils of war?" Her smile irritated me. I knew it was sarcastic.

I was determined to ignore her, but clearly Patrice wanted to talk about something. What now? "Again, what do you need?"

Her sad smile revealed her disappointment. Huh. Maybe she did want to chat? "Why are you suspicious of everything? I haven't seen you much since you started working. We used to hang out a lot more. And..." she added as she tugged on a tassel of my favorite throw pillow. "Mom and Dad say that you refuse to change your major."

Patrice enjoyed the fact that I had chosen a major that irritated our parents. She of course was attending Springhill College, Mobile's most elite school, and majoring in nursing. The perfect daughter, never straying too far from the path that Mom and Dad had set out for her when she was born. Straight-A student at St. Mary's and McGill, graduating with honors. You name it, Patrice did it and excelled. I marveled that Mom and Dad even noticed me at all. She could probably be a doctor—she had the brains for it—but that wasn't what our parents wanted, so she didn't even think about it.

"I'm sticking with art history. Did they send you in here? That's pretty crappy, Patrice."

She whacked me with the pillow. "You know how much they loathe the idea of spending money on a humanities degree. Why don't you just change it and be done with it? It would make them happy, and since they are footing the bill...."

*But it wouldn't make me happy, and that's the point. Isn't it? We are so different. I love her, but it's like we are night and day. Maybe I'm adopted.*

"They aren't footing my bill, Patrice. I've taken out student loans, and as soon as I'm able, I'm moving out." Huh, I hadn't really decided on that last part, but I was pretty angry at the moment. Imagine the nerve of my parents, trying to control me like that. "It's not about what makes them happy, Patrice. It's about what I want to do with my life. You should think about that yourself. It's your life, sister. Why do you let them control you like that? What happened to your dancing? You used to love it."

She stared at me with her beautiful green eyes. It was a sad, kind of blank stare. I swear those words must seem foreign to her. I had to give it to her—she really wanted to make our parental units happy. I did too, but not like her.

"I did that. I danced all through school. Dancing won't bring me a solid future, Aggie. I am thinking about the future. What will you do with an art history degree?"

"Enjoy my life."

She rose from the bed and shook her head. "Okay, well, you still have time to change your mind."

Seriously, it was like talking to a brick wall. "Give it up, Patrice. Just drop it. Did they send you in here? So much for sisterhood."

"No," Patrice replied nervously, "they didn't. I'm trying to keep the peace." Her response meant that they most certainly did send her in here.

"Well, I'm not changing my mind," I huffed back.

"So, what is this, anyway?" she asked as she walked around to the nightstand. She picked up the dainty cup and examined it. I knew she was changing the subject, but I didn't want to answer the question. Why did she have to pry into my business?

"It's a teacup, obviously." I hesitated, then added, "From the antiques shop."

Patrice interrupted, "Did you steal this? Aggie! Tell me you paid for it! You have to take it back. What would Mom and Dad say? They would be so embarrassed if they found out that you..."

"Patrice! I didn't steal it," I shot back. The nerve of her accusing me. I'm a lot of things, but a thief? No way. Not unless you count a pack of gum. Only once, when I was in the fifth grade. And Patrice dared me to do it! Had she forgotten all about that?

"You better be telling the truth."

"Are you through? One minute I'm the family failure, the next I'm a thief? When will it end?" I asked as I rose from the bed with my arms crossed. If she wanted a fight, I'd give her one.

To my complete surprise, my sister grabbed me and hugged me. "Sorry. I'm sorry for intimating that you'd steal a cup. I'm just...I'm your sister, and I want what's best for you." Patrice laughed, and I sank a bit in her arms. Despite my stubborn attitude, I hugged her back. "You wanna go grab some coffee or something?" she asked.

I did miss hanging out with her, but I wanted to find out more about the cup.

"Sure, just give me about half an hour?"

"I guess I can do that," she replied, smiling at me as she left the room.

A few minutes should give me enough time to go into my vision. Surely, I could make this all work out. Spending time with my sister meant the world to me. I knew we wouldn't have much quality time together with us attending different schools this fall.

I picked up the cup and took a deep breath. This needed to be done, right? I mean, I needed to find out what Bette wanted to say. *Okay, Aggie, you can do this. Just relax.*

Concentrating on the image of the two young women that I had seen before and holding the cup tightly in my hands, I waited.

Taking a few more deep breaths, I slid into the vision. *Yes, I am here.* I made it back to that moment. The young women sat like two dolls, poised on the edge of conversation. Frozen in time.

Waiting.

*Waiting for me.*

The smell of clove hit me, and I knew that I was settling into the scene again. They were sitting in the same spot where I had left them before, the blonde on one side and the dark-haired woman on the other. Bette's anxiety—I experienced it. And the other girl, she had lovely dark hair; she wore it swept up into an elegant bun. It was a style that should be too old and sophisticated for her, but Rosalie was lovely.

*Rosalie…that's her name.*

The dark-haired woman, Rosalie, swirled the cup around, making the gold trim of the cup sparkle in the dim light. I tried to make out what they were saying to each other, but their voices were too low.

Studying their features was all I could do, and I hoped something could give me a hint about where the lost cup might be. Had she taken it, stolen it back through time? *How ridiculous! No, stupid. Pay attention.* I reminded myself to keep my wits about me. I leaned in, mesmerized by the scene.

Rosalie glanced up from the cup. Her face was filled with confusion as she focused on Bette. There were tears in her eyes.

"What is it?" Bette whispered, but it was barely intelligible. They sounded as if they were underwater. Deep underwater.

I couldn't believe it, but I heard her! *Yes, what is it*, I thought. *What is it, Rosalie?*

She mumbled something, but whatever it was, I couldn't understand her. It was infuriating. I wanted to find out what was going on. Something was there for me to find out, but what was it? Why could I hear Bette but not Rosalie? What was she hiding?

"What is it?" I shouted out loud at her. I just couldn't take it anymore.

Rosalie began to speak. "Bette, there seems to be a great deal of confusion in your future. You will be happy but restless," she said, looking into the teacup.

"Restless?" Bette asked.

Rosalie picked up a dark brown cigarette and took a drag. "You will marry this man and have children with him, but you will feel like something is missing. This is just the path that you will have to take."

The unmistakable scent of clove hit me. Was she smoking clove cigarettes? That must be why that smell kept popping up.

Bette seemed even more anxious.

*No wonder people don't do tea reading much anymore; it wasn't very clear. I mean, who isn't restless in their lives?*

"Rosalie, is that all you see?" Bette asked.

She looked up from the teacup with concern. "Bette, there is more. My life is in danger. Someone wants to get rid of me for good. Do you understand?"

Bette shook her head slowly, her face glistening with tears. "Who, Rosalie? Who would want to hurt you?"

"I wish I could tell you, but I'm afraid it would only make matters worse," Rosalie solemnly replied.

"Please tell me. Maybe I could stop them."

Before Rosalie could speak, another woman entered the room. I had never seen this person before. Not another mysterious woman. She was older than Bette and Rosalie and looked much more proper than either one of them. Her hair was pulled back away from her face. It was a hairstyle that she must have gone to the hairstylist each week to maintain. She was dressed way better than I would ever dream of, and it looked like she would die rather than wear jeans. Her demeanor reminded me of the wicked stepmother in a Disney film.

Rosalie dropped the cup she was holding and chipped it on the table.

*So that's how it happened.*

Who was this lady, and why was Rosalie afraid of her?

"Mother..." Bette said.

"What is *she* doing here?" the woman replied, looking down her nose at Rosalie. "You know how I feel about such things, Bette. How dare you use my mother's tea set to do such evil things? And now look at what she's done! She's broken it with her witchcraft! What if someone finds out? Don't you care anything about our family name?"

Wow, this sounded familiar. She sounded just like Patrice.

"Mother, I didn't mean to..."

Bette's mother interrupted, "You never do. I want her out of this house now. Preferably out the back door, and make sure no one sees her."

A pained expression fell on Rosalie's face as she glanced over at Bette. I could feel their emotions and became overwhelmed with sadness. These two had a connection.

Rosalie put out her cigarette, taking Bette's hands in hers and squeezing them tightly. "Bette, I'm sorry for the trouble I've caused." She turned toward Bette's mom and added, "Mrs. Hollingsworth, it was nice seeing you again."

Mrs. Hollingsworth's face screwed up, and her eyes narrowed into a demonic-looking mask. Pure evil.

I squeezed the cup tighter in my hands.

"Aggie! What are you doing?" a familiar voice yelled back at me, snapping me out of my vision. I almost dropped the cup. I slowly opened my eyes.

Standing in front of me was Patrice. There was no getting around it. She caught me in the middle of my vision. How was I going to talk my way out of this one?

"What are you doing in here?" I asked, panicked.

"Don't put this on me, Mary Agnes! What are *you* doing with that?" Patrice shouted as she snatched the cup from my hands and put it on the nightstand with the saucer. There was no way out of this. I had to tell her what was going on. This wasn't the way I wanted to tell my sister, but here we were and I had no way out.

"Patrice, you need to sit down." I rubbed at the tears in my eyes.

She slowly walked toward me and sat beside me on the bed. "What is it? There's no excuse for this. I know what you're doing."

"You can't possibly know. I'll tell you, but you have to promise me that you won't freak out."

There was no way she wasn't going to freak out. Patrice was the normal one. She didn't believe in anything like this. The idea of having a sister with psychic abilities was totally going to make her flip. I was sure this would go over like a lead balloon.

"I'm not sure I can promise that," Patrice popped back, but her hands were shaking and her green eyes wide.

I grabbed both of her hands. "I can *see* dead people. When I touch things that belong to them, I can see them. Sometimes. It's not a perfect science, but I'm learning. Trust me. I'm telling the absolute truth."

She snatched her hands away. "Stop joking around, Mary Agnes. What were you doing? Are you on drugs or something?"

"No! Come on, Patrice, I'm serious!" She was seriously not getting it or not wanting to.

"Okay, okay, okay...ummmm..." Patrice was pacing back and forth in front of my bed now, trying to take in what I told her. Rubbing her hands together and flipping out, like I knew she would.

"Sit back down," I said as I fell back on my pillow. "Please. You're making it worse."

"Worse? How am I making it worse? I swear, Aggie! Why can't you just be normal! I'm so tired of covering for you!"

Wow. That stung. "I'm telling you the truth. When I hold certain objects, I can see spirits and how they used the object. Not all the time but sometimes. It's like a vision of sorts. I can also detect scents connected with people who've passed."

Patrice sat there staring past me. At least she'd stopped pacing the floor. I wasn't sure what to expect now. I sat there, waiting and hoping she would say something useful. She didn't. "Patrice, you have to promise me that you won't tell them. I'll tell Mom and Dad soon enough, in my own time. But right now, I need you to keep this between us."

Still silent, she just nodded.

I would tell my parents, but I needed to work up the nerve. They would be even worse than Patrice, and the thought that they might commit me did cross my mind. Maybe not, but the possibility was rather high. Telling them this would be the nail in my abnormal coffin. The parentals already thought I was strange; this would put them over the edge.

Finally, Patrice spoke. "Okay, I won't tell them as long as you promise me that *you* will."

"I promise," I answered glumly. "What's the worst that can happen?"

Patrice bit her fingernail. That was her one bad habit. This wasn't good. "When did this first start? How did you know it was spirits you were seeing and not just some dream or something?"

"I've been able to do this all my life, but recently it's picked up strength. Especially since I started working at the antiques shop."

"That's why you have the cup?" Patrice asked. "You did this intentionally?"

I hesitated for a minute. Should I tell her anything? "Yes, but that's all I'm going to say."

"Oh my goodness, Aggie, you are trying to speak with the dead in our house! This is too much. I just can't..."

"Patty, you've got to calm down," I interrupted.

"How can I calm down? This is NOT normal!"

*Great, now she freaks out. Of course it's not normal, it's me. I'm not normal. She's definitely gonna tell our parents.*

"Look! I know it's not normal. That's why I haven't ever told all you normal people. You've got to keep quiet."

She took a few deep breaths. "Okay, I'm calm. I'm going to leave, and we are going to have coffee. We are NOT going to discuss this anymore, and mum's the word to our parents. I can't tell them something like this. They would FREAK out." Patrice left my room shaking her head.

This was terrible. I never should have taken the cup and saucer out of the shop. I had to get it back there as soon as possible. Patrice promised she wouldn't blab, but she couldn't help but be the favorite. She had never lied to the parentals, never held anything back. There's no way she could keep a secret like this.

And here's what blew: I was not any closer to finding out what happened between Bette and Rosalie, and now my sister knew about me.

*What will I tell my parents?*

I quietly traipsed down the stairs and joined Patrice at the breakfast table. Then we sat there at the coffee shop ignoring the elephant in the room. Patrice looked away from me as she drank her coffee. Two sugars, one cream. It was always the same. She never tried anything different. It was exactly how our mother drank it.

I broke the silence, "Are we going to talk about it?"

"Nope," Patrice replied without even looking my way.

"Look…"

"I said no," Patrice interrupted, giving me the stare of hate. That's what I called that look when we were kids. But we weren't kids anymore. We were young women. Sisters. We should be able to share things like this.

"But…"

"No!"

I sat back in my chair and took a sip of coffee. I preferred tea, but I wasn't in a position to complain. No one else in the family drank Earl Grey but me. Oddball through and through. I couldn't help but think about my vision. It would be nice to be able to talk to Patrice about it, but there she sat across from her weirdo sister, blocking it all out.

"I just want to say one thing," I whispered quickly.

She looked over at me and let me continue.

"I'm not sure how this all works, but I'm trying to help someone. This isn't just for funsies. I need you to understand that this is just who I am."

Patrice turned toward me. "I understand. I always try to understand your quirks, but this is different. You are talking to spirits in our home, and that could cause a lot of problems. Don't open that door, Aggie. You could let in something that you don't want to let in. You know how religious Mom and Dad are, Aggie. If they knew, they would freak out even more than me. It's not right, Mary Agnes."

Her words made my insides flip. She was serious and seemed really concerned. I knew she wouldn't be able to keep something like this from our parents forever. How could she? She was the poster child, and I was the sidekick. The one with occasional acne and a bad singing voice.

"I'm not summoning anything, Patrice, if that's what you're thinking. You think what I do will draw attention from the spirit world, but you've got it all wrong. They are already here. They are always with us. I can't continue to ignore them, to ignore my gift. I can't. I won't."

"Fine. Do what you want, but you better tell Mom and Dad what you're up to." With a clink of her cup on her saucer, she left me alone to stare out the window. At least it was a pretty day out.

I didn't have long before she told on me. That much was for sure. Strangely enough, I didn't hate her for it. I loved her and understood her fear. I sighed and sipped my coffee, wondering when the ball would drop.

Yep. It was only a matter of time.

## Chapter Eight—Bette

The house shook again, and the air positively vibrated with electricity. I could not take my eyes off Rosalie, who sat as still as a statue. Her red lips quivered, or perhaps it was merely an illusion caused by the flickering candlelight. Her confession hung in the air between us, and strangely enough, I believed her. I couldn't account for such trust and belief, yet I certainly did believe the dark-haired teen. I searched her face for clues. Yes, we were similar in appearance, but they weren't obvious similarities. She had dark eyes and hair, as dark as I was frighteningly pale and blond. Yes, we both had that strange nervous tic; our lips were a dead giveaway. Mine quivered too when I was nervous or worried.

My reaction was not normal. I should be shocked—appalled, even—by Rosalie's claim. I remembered my mother pelting me with questions, not just about Rosalie but about a few other girls in my graduating class. I thought it odd at the time, but Mother had spells like that. She had to know everything about everyone all the time. It was exhausting trying to satisfy her incessant need to know every move I made, every conversation I had. Even the most unimportant exchange, such as my greeting the mailman's wife at the grocery store, worried her no end. But more than once she had quizzed me about Rosalie; she'd even warned me to avoid her because of some sort of gossip she'd overheard at one of her society meetings.

Mother repeatedly asked questions about her like, "What was she wearing?" or "What did she say?" and "How did she say it?"

I assured her we never spoke. Still, Mother displayed periods of paranoia and a level of calculation that disturbed me. At least it wasn't only focused on Rosalie. Mother was suspicious about everyone—even the school's most popular girl, Hannah Mayfair. I would much rather enjoy the company of my schoolmates and my few friends without worrying about collecting gossip for Mother. Yes, she thought herself very important and believed that everyone was out to get her. Not me so much. I was not that important, but the Hollingsworth name—she revered it beyond reason. Never mind that I was also a Hollingsworth.

"Did you hear me, Bette? I am your sister. I wanted you to know before I left Mobile."

"Yes, I heard you." My voice sounded hollow, kind of empty. It was as if I always knew it. Rosalie *was* my sister—my own flesh and blood. For years, I had pined for a sister, which flabbergasted Mother. "You're leaving Mobile? Really?"

"I can't stay here. She'll never leave me alone, Bette. You have to know that."

"I always knew I had a sister. Somehow, I knew." Memories of an old argument with Mother replayed in my mind.

*Are you sure, Mother? I would love to have someone to play with!*

*Don't be a fool, Bette. Your father is dead. It would be quite impossible to have another child.*

That had been the conversation we'd had. It had been my fifth birthday. I'd blown out the candles and made my wish. Naturally, I wished for a sister, and later that evening my inquisitive, nosy mother pushed me to tell her what exactly I wished for. That had been a big mistake. A very big mistake. I would never forget how enraged she'd become over such a statement.

"You don't seem surprised, Bette," Rosalie answered in a tense yet sad voice. She set a small purse down on the table, a fabric purse with a heavy golden chain and colorful blue tassels. Without another word, she opened the purse and removed a brass cigarette case. She opened it with a snap and took out a dark-colored cigarette, then flicked a lighter and lit the cigarette. The spicy aroma of clove filled the kitchen in just a few puffs. Mother would not be happy about this; smoking in her beautiful home was blasphemous.

"May I have one?" I asked as I breathed in the delightful smell. Rosalie appeared so sophisticated holding her slender cigarette gingerly in one hand.

"Sure." She handed me a cigarette and flicked the lighter for me.

"I knew I had a sister. I always knew." I coughed and sputtered as I breathed in the smoke of the harsh clove cigarette. Ew. My first cigarette was not an enjoyable experience. "How could she keep that from me? I don't understand, unless it's her pride. She's a proud woman."

"I assume you are speaking of Mrs. Hollingsworth. It is complicated for her, I think. My mother said…well, I do not want to speak ill of your mother even though she has no love for me. She has been very protective of you. I have been here before, Bette."

"What?"

Rosalie puffed on her cigarette again, and I mimicked her even though doing so made me cough. My lungs burned, my heart raced, and I knew I'd catch what-for from Mother—she'd smell the cigarette smoke when she returned home. But I had this moment. I felt like an enchanted rabbit. I can't say why that particular description came to mind. I was riveted by Rosalie's confession and her beauty and everything about her.

"What do you mean? How does she know you, Rosalie? I guess this means my father—I mean, your father—they are one and the same? Is that right? Am I the oldest? Was your mother his first wife? I never knew…I mean, you have to believe me…I did not know."

"No, Bette. You are the oldest. One year older."

"Oh," was all I could stammer out as I put the smoking cigarette on the saucer. I lost my appetite for smoking. My mind raced with the implications of Rosalie's confession. That means Father had been unfaithful to Mother. That he'd loved another and

*A Cup of Shadows*

that he'd known I had a sister and never told me. Wait! Maybe he did not know after all. This was too much to think about. Far too much!

"I can't understand why they wouldn't tell me. I should have been told." I got up from the chair and began wringing my hands as I paced the kitchen. The storm continued to rage outside, and I was near to tears. I had no idea how to describe the cacophony of emotions that roiled beneath the surface of my skin.

*I knew! I always knew!*

Rosalie watched me from behind a cloud of cigarette smoke. "Don't worry so. I do not expect anything. I do not want anything from you, Bette. You do not have to do anything at all. I wanted you to know the truth—you truly are my sister."

"You must want something. Why else would you tell me this, Rosalie?" I asked as I chewed my fingernail and collapsed in the chair across from her. "Is it money? Mother never gives me any, if that's what you're after." I could not account for the sudden anger I had for my new sister.

Rosalie put her cigarette in the saucer alongside mine. She reached across the table and touched my hand carefully. "I do not want anything, sister. If I may call you that. Only to tell you the truth before I leave here forever." Again I detected her strange accent. She must work hard at hiding it, but on occasion it oozed forth, warm and comforting. "Maybe to do one more thing for you."

"I don't understand. Why do you have to leave?"

She sighed, and despite her lovely youthful appearance, Rosalie suddenly seemed like an old soul with her expressive eyes. By candlelight, the dark circles beneath them were easy to see. She did not look well, so frail and fragile like an injured bird. I wondered if her mother had had lovely eyes too. Perhaps that's why Father fell in love with another woman. Perhaps those dark eyes captured his heart. Did he ever love Mother? Did he ever love me?

"For more reasons than I can explain to you, Bette. It is best for everyone. Better for you, better for me. Your mother barely tolerated my existence before. With no one to have a care for me, I fear she will do everything she can to make life hard for me. I have a little money, and the whole world is before me. There is nothing to keep me here."

"I don't want you to go, Rosalie. I am sorry about what I said. I just need time to think. Time to make sense of all this."

Rosalie smiled sadly. "You do not have time. I am sorry for that. I wasn't sure."

"Wasn't sure of what, Rosalie?"

"I wasn't sure that you didn't know about me. Sometimes...I have seen you watch me. I have seen you, and I thought maybe you did know and wanted to keep it a secret. I cannot say I blame you."

I blushed at hearing her thoughts. How could I ever pretend that Rosalie was not my sister? I would not do that, but she was correct in believing it would cause a scandal. A terrible scandal for the Hollingsworth name. "I did not know a thing, I assure you." I wiped at a tear with my free hand as Rosalie continued to gently hold the other. "Like I said, I guess I always knew. Always. We do favor each other, don't we? We are truly sisters. I will speak to my mother. I will make her accept you. I swear it, Rosalie."

Rosalie withdrew her hand and shook her head slowly. "No, Bette. She knows already. She knows and hates me—just as she hated my mother. Mrs. Hollingsworth has been to our house many times. She even offered us money to leave, but Mama never wanted to leave Mobile. She believed that eventually your mother would come around and accept me. That she would allow us to be sisters, but I always knew it would not happen. And now Mama is gone. I have made my peace with it all. But you, Bette, I am sorry."

"Please, don't leave yet. I want to get to know you."

"I will write to you. I will share with you all of my adventures, and maybe one day you can join me."

"Where will you go, Rosalie?"

She smiled, and her eyes brightened. "California. I long to see the ocean."

"You can see the ocean here," I pleaded with her. "We are only a half-hour away from the Gulf of Mexico, Rosalie. We could go together."

"Not the Gulf but the Pacific Ocean. My father, our father, used to tell me about it. He loved California and the waters there. I want to go see that ocean. I need to go."

The lights flickered on and then off again. The storm's power decreased. The lightning flashed sporadically, but the storm moved on rather quickly.

"I want to do something for you, Bette. Drink your tea. I can read your leaves—I'll tell you what I see. My mother taught me how to interpret them."

"She did? You mean she was a tea reader?"

"Mama did many things. Read cards, leaves and palms. She was a good woman. You believe me, don't you? You won't let your mother convince you otherwise?" It was Rosalie's turn to shed a tear. She wiped it away, and now I reached across the table and comforted her by holding her hand.

"I won't believe her, Rosalie. Promise me you will stay in touch. I want to know you, to talk to you often. Promise you will write?"

"I do promise."

My mind raced with the possibilities. I could not allow her to send mail to this address because I was certain Mother would intervene. We would have to figure that out. Maybe the neighbor would allow Rosalie to send a letter to me at her address? I could ask. I would certainly ask. I was old enough to get a postal box, but Mother would find out. It was impossible to keep secrets from her.

"Now sip your tea, Bette. I cannot leave without seeing for myself. I have to know you will be safe. I must know."

I did not understand any of this, but I did as she asked. I sipped the tea and left a swallow in the bottom, along with a few loose tea leaves. The lights flickered on as Rosalie accepted the teacup from my shaking hands. Were there tears in her eyes?

"What is it?" I asked, my heart pounding.

Finally, she began to speak. "Bette, there seems to be a great deal of confusion in your future. You will be happy but restless," she said, looking into the teacup.

"Restless?"

"You will marry this man and have children with him, but you will feel like something is missing. This is just the path that you will have to take."

"Rosalie, is that all you see?" I asked.

She looked up from the teacup with concern. "Bette, there is more. My life is in danger. Someone wants to get rid of me for good. Do you understand?"

I shook my head in disbelief. "Who, Rosalie? Who would want to hurt you?"

"I wish I could tell you, but I'm afraid it would only make matters worse."

"Please tell me. Maybe I could stop them."

But before she could tell me, she looked up and dropped the cup, chipping it. I turned around, knowing who stood behind me.

"Mother..."

"What is *she* doing here?" my mother spat out. "You know how I feel about such things, Bette. How dare you use my mother's tea set to do such evil things? And now look at what she's done! She's broken it with her witchcraft! What if someone finds out? Don't you care anything about our family name?"

## Chapter Nine—Aggie

This cup and saucer had caused me enough problems, and I was happy to get it back to the shop. The only thing now was I had to sneak it back in without the Boss Lady and Henri finding out I took it. That's all I needed. I was in enough hot water at home with Patrice.

I wanted to help, but I'd crossed the line by taking the cup and saucer home...and I paid dearly for it. What made me think that Patrice wouldn't come barging into my room unannounced? She never respected my privacy before. I sure didn't get why she felt the need to be so nosy. Pulling up to the shop, I noticed that the parking lot was empty. Hopefully, no one was inside yet. I purposefully came a little early just to return these things.

Putting my key into the door, I slowly opened it and waited for any sound of human life. It was a relief when I was met with silence. I let out the breath that I had been holding and walked over to the table where the rest of the set was displayed.

Before I could get the saucer out of my bag, I heard a noise. It sounded like singing. That couldn't be Detra Ann. She never sang in the shop. I don't even think she would sing by herself much less in front of anyone. I put the saucer back in my bag and walked toward the back of the shop. The singing stopped as I got closer.

"Hello," I called and waited for a response.

The shop fell silent again. No one else was there but me. Maybe it was someone outside? We did have a lot of foot traffic out on the street some mornings. Strange. I didn't see anyone strolling around when I pulled up. I walked back to the front and peeked out the door. Nope. Not a dang thing. I raced to the back again and quickly put the saucer and cup on the table, wanting to get rid of the cursed things. This whole experiment had been a nightmare.

The soft singing began again when I took my hand away from the cup and then faded as quickly as it started. *Okay, Mary Agnes, get a grip. This has to be my imagination.* But despite my sensible reasoning, I couldn't shake the feeling that someone was in the shop with me.

"Detra Ann? Henri?"

I froze, unable to move away from the tea set. It felt like there was some invisible force holding me there. I wanted to run, but my legs just wouldn't move. The singing started again. I could almost make out the words. A feminine sing-songy voice that was kind of familiar. Kind of.

"Hello?"

All I heard were unintelligible whispers.

Now whispering voices? What in the world was happening?

A whiff of clove moved past my face. I knew this fragrance well. It had been a part of my vision! Yes, it smelled like one of those clove cigarettes. My grandma used to smoke them on occasion too, so it's not like I'd never smelled them before. That kind of memory doesn't fade. No one in the shop smoked, so I knew it wasn't one of us. Maybe a customer? There was no way Detra Ann would allow smoking around all these fine things.

Who could it be? The scent left just as quickly as it had arrived, and the singing went away too. I had to be losing my mind.

"Is anyone there?" I whispered, hoping no one would answer.

"Aggie?" Detra Ann's voice came from behind me. I jumped about a foot off the ground. "What are you doing?" she said with a nervous laugh. I tried to answer her, but the words just wouldn't come out of my mouth. "Are you okay?" The look of concern on her face made me feel guilty. "You didn't hear me come in?"

"Yes," I managed to squeak out. "I mean, no."

Detra Ann wasn't convinced. "You don't look okay. You look like you've seen a ghost. What's going on, Aggie?" Before I could answer, the singing returned and I didn't have to say a thing. "Is there a customer in the store?" Detra Ann asked.

"No. I don't think so. I just opened the shop. You hear it too?" I continued to whisper.

"Yes. Why are we whispering? Is someone here or not?"

I shook my head slowly. "I don't think so." We stood there looking at each other, unsure of what to do. Then the scent hit me again. "Do you smell that? It's clove. From a cigarette." I hoped that she did indeed smell it. I sniffed the air again to make sure. It was definitely clove. My heart was racing like a train driven by a maniacal engineer.

Detra Ann took a few deep breaths. "It is clove. Was someone smoking in the shop yesterday? Are you sure no one is here?" She walked around the front room, and I stuck close to her. There was no way anyone snuck in here. No way at all. I didn't even have the lights on yet.

"No. I didn't see anyone, and that's not all. There was singing too—it was coming from upstairs. I have to tell you something else." I swallowed as I steeled myself for what I was about to do.

"What is it, Aggie?"

"I took one of the cups and a matching saucer to my house last night. I thought I could use them to connect. I can't really explain it all. It sounds crazy, but it's true. I've returned them, but I just wanted to let you know. I think that may have something to do with the clove scent and the singing."

Detra Ann turned her pretty head at an inquisitive angle. "Why? What do you mean that you could use them to connect? Did you see my friend? Did you connect with Bette? You're talking about what you mentioned before. Psychometry?"

"Right, but as it turns out, I'm not very good at it. I tried. I did see her, and she wasn't alone. Her sister was there. Her name is Rosalie. She told Bette that something was going to happen to her if she didn't leave Mobile. Someone wanted to hurt Rosalie."

It was nice being able to talk openly to someone about all of this. Detra Ann believed me and didn't think I was strange. For once, I didn't feel like an oddball. But before I could spill my guts—and believe me, I wanted to do just that—we heard the singing again. It was coming from upstairs, and I could hear footsteps. Light footsteps, like a child or a petite woman was walking in the apartment above us.

"Did you hear that?" I whispered to her, but she was already making her way to the front door and flipped the closed sign back around. She locked the door and then dug in her purse for her keys. "Detra Ann? Is it Henri? I haven't been up in the storage area. Who is that?"

"I don't know. Grab the phone and the bat, Aggie."

"Bat?" I asked stupidly as I reached for the phone.

"The small one behind the counter. Shoot! I knew I should have kept a gun up here." Detra Ann began walking to the doorway that led upstairs and unlocked it.

That's right, I remembered the miniature bat now. "Wait! Are we going up there?"

"I am, at least. I can't sit back and do nothing while someone plunders around up there. Are you with me?"

"Is there another way in? Could someone have broken in? Should we call the cops or something? I think we should let them handle it, Boss Lady."

"There is a door that leads straight up to the apartment, but I have a padlock on it. I parked around back, so if the door were open I would have noticed." The footsteps continued—there was no denying that someone was upstairs. I had chills all over my body. "Keep the phone handy. If we need to call the cops, we will sooner rather than later. Stay close."

With a determined expression, Detra Ann opened the door. I followed behind her as we ascended into the darkness.

Gritting my teeth, I clutched the bat with purpose.

## Chapter Ten—Detra Ann

"Hello? Who's up here? I heard you, so there's no sense in hiding. My friend and I have weapons." I swayed on my feet as I jangled the keys in my hand. Suddenly I had the bright idea to arrange them so they poked out from my fist like shanks. If I had to defend us and protect my property in a forceful way, I would certainly do so.

"You can't hide from us," I continued as I flipped on the light switch. "This is my place—my store. Come out now and I won't call the cops." I waited for an answer and waved at Aggie to keep her beside me. Dang overhead light didn't come on. Had the bulb blown? Was there a problem with the wiring? I didn't smell wires burning, nothing to indicate that there was an actual electrical problem. I scurried to the sofa table and flipped the lamp switch, but it did not turn on either. What was going on up here? The breaker must have flipped. Shoot. The breaker was downstairs in the store closet.

I did smell clove cigarettes. Aggie wasn't a smoker—I'd never seen her smoking or vaping or doing anything like that. "I don't see anyone," Aggie whispered into the darkness. As quick as lightning, she hurried to the far window and pulled up the blinds. I breathed a sigh of relief as light filled the room. "Still no one." Immediately she ran down the hall and went to explore the other rooms.

"Aggie! Wait!" I raced after her.

There were two bedrooms and a bathroom down that hall. Henri and I lived here for a while before we bought our house, and he had definitely been keen on renting the place out these days, just for some extra income, to kind of defray the store overhead. Me? Not so much. This comfy apartment had too many good memories for me. Memories I did not want to share with an intrusive stranger. Yep, this place had been so wonderful. Until we outgrew it. Until our daughter came along.

As I joined Aggie in the master bedroom, I didn't see anything out of place. The room was empty except for an extremely heavy chest of drawers, too heavy for Henri and me to move. It was easily the largest thing left in the apartment. Aggie checked out the closet, but it was empty too. Whoever we'd heard walking around up here didn't want to be found. The hair on my arms raised up as I pondered the meaning of all this. What in heaven's name was happening up here?

"You hear that?" Aggie asked me, poised with the bat in her hand. "Whispers. I hear people talking."

I would like to have denied that I heard anything at all, but that wasn't possible because I did hear two soft voices talking rapidly but too quietly to understand. I couldn't hear what they were saying, but the tone led me to believe it was important.

"It's Bette and Rosalie. They were sisters, Detra Ann. But they didn't know it for a long time. I think we should keep looking." And with that, she was gone again. Her Vans made light tapping sounds on the wooden floors as she sped off to the second bedroom, the bathroom and then back to the living area.

"Aggie, you can't run off like that. We have to stick together. Trust me on this. I know a little about ghost hunting."

"Then you do think we're hearing ghosts. Bette's ghost? Do you think it's really her?"

"Oh my gosh! Look, Aggie. Is that what I think it is?" I walked into the kitchen. We'd left a small table in the dining area, which was essentially the corner of the kitchen. On top of the table was a jar candle and the missing cup and saucer. I couldn't believe it. "How did they get up here? It is definitely the cup and saucer from the set. Same color and design, same gold rim."

"Don't look at me, Detra Ann. I didn't bring them up here. You know I don't have a key. Please, believe me. You have to believe me."

Before I could quiz her further, the apartment door squeaked open and Henri's handsome face appeared. "What are y'all doing up here? We've got customers trying to get in and the appraiser is here. You two okay?"

It was hard to pretend that everything was okay, but I slapped a smile on my face. "We're looking around. We found the cup and saucer set. I think I must have brought it up here and forgotten about it. That's the only thing I can figure. But we found it, so that will make Mr. Ladner happy."

"Nice place. I got the full tour today," Aggie said as she glanced at me. "It's roomier than I thought."

Henri flashed his beautiful, perfect smile. I swear, that man was so gorgeous. Inside and out. "Hey, are you looking for an apartment? Detra Ann and I were talking about renting it out. It might be too much for just one person, though. I guess you could bring in a roommate. Is that what you're thinking, sweetheart?"

I couldn't believe my ears. How on earth had he come to that conclusion? But it wasn't a bad idea. I liked Aggie, even though I didn't know her that well. She'd certainly passed my lie detector tests.

"Um, I think that's a possibility. Mind if I take a few pictures?"

"Sure," Henri agreed. "Take all the time you need, but it looks like it might be a busy day. I think those ads are doing the trick. Good job on that, by the way. In case we haven't told you already. I'll take the cup and saucer downstairs, if you like. Detra Ann, will you help me? Mrs. Zirlott is here for that horrible purple desk."

"Of course. I'll bring the dishes, Harry. You go sweet-talk Mrs. Zirlott and see if she'll take that mirror too."

"Great," he groaned. I knew he wasn't excited about the idea of flirting with the overly friendly Mrs. Zirlott, but as he mentioned frequently, we needed the sales.

Henri hurried down the stairs, and I paused to whisper, "Thanks for covering for me. You know, it's not a bad idea, if you're interested in the apartment."

"You mean once we get the ghosts out. How about letting me bring the cup and saucer down? I swear I won't lose them. If I could have just a minute with them, that would be great. I think I could really connect with Bette and Rosalie. They want to tell me something, I just know it."

"Are you sure?" I asked with some hesitation. Ghosts were unpredictable, and many of them were not friendly. I'd feel horrible if Aggie got hurt.

I didn't need one more thing on my conscience. Not one more thing. I could barely afford my sessions with Dr. Kepler already. Losing TD, my past alcohol abuse and my relationships were enough to talk about. I didn't want to blame myself for any other tragedies.

But her pleading expression left me no choice. I had to trust her. I had to give her a chance to listen to the voices we'd both heard. Poor Bette. She'd left us too soon.

"Five minutes, Aggie. Please, don't do anything stupid."

"Never. Five minutes is all I need."

I watched with some hesitation as she sat down at the rickety table, the cup and saucer before her.

I hoped this wasn't five minutes that I'd regret forever.

## *Chapter Eleven—Aggie*

What was Rosalie going to tell Bette before Mrs. Hollingsworth walked in? She'd already blown my mind by confessing that she was Bette's sister. Why was she crying when she read her tea leaves? I needed more time to find out what happened. Thank goodness Detra Ann let me stay behind and seek answers.

Holding the chipped cup in my hands, I reminded myself to relax and let go of the present. *Think about the cup, think about only the cup.* I waited impatiently for my perception to shift.

It didn't take long. The vision began right away. Yes, I could see! Only this time, the beautiful, sad-faced Rosalie was absent from the scene. It was Bette's mother in the kitchen with the young blonde. I smothered a gasp as Mrs. Hollingsworth slapped her with an open hand. Bette whimpered as she collapsed onto the floor without so much as a yelp. Her shoulders sagged in defeat.

"Why did you invite that witch into our house, Bette? You fool! Do you know what you've done?" Mrs. Hollingsworth clutched the side of the sink, her chest heaving as if she were the one who had been struck.

"I didn't invite her, Mother, and she's not a witch. She just stopped by to say hello, that's all. Rosalie has been lonely since her mother passed. I know her from school."

"Good riddance to bad rubbish!" Mrs. Hollingsworth muttered as she made her way to a chair. Bette cautiously sat in the chair across from her.

"No, please!" Bette warned defiantly. "You shouldn't speak that way about the dead." Bette bit her lip but continued, "She told me...I know the truth, Mother. I know who she is—who I am!"

"What truth?" her mother barked back. "What do you think you know?"

Bette didn't answer and even turned her face away.

"Good riddance to her, I say. And I can speak however I want in my own house, Bette Hollingsworth. I don't care how old you get, you'll never be the boss of me, daughter of mine. I can see how that Rosalie has influenced you already. She is never to come back here. That girl is not welcome." Mrs. Hollingsworth lifted her pinky as she brought the teacup to her wrinkled lips with shaky fingers. She set the cup back to the saucer, her lips parted in a hard slit. "This is how it will be."

"How can you be so heartless? You knew all this time."

Mrs. Hollingsworth was not moved by Bette's broken voice. "Never let her darken my doorway again."

"You don't have to worry about her coming around, Mother. Rosalie is leaving Mobile." Bette's shoulders slouched slightly. Her normally poised demeanor vanished, and I could feel her sadness like my very own.

"Oh, I don't worry about her, dear. The gypsy in her won't allow her to stay in one place for too long. Good thing, too. People like that tend to just *disappear*."

Her words lingered in the air like a heavy threat. An odd thing to say, wasn't it?

Bette was so sweet, but her mother made my blood turn cold. The image of the two women began to float away like smoke. For the first time, I knew what message was clearly given.

Detra Ann was pacing around the room when I came out of my vision. "We need to talk," I said as I wiped my palms on my jeans. I wasn't sure how to tell her what I was feeling, but she would find out eventually. You couldn't hide anything from her.

"What's going on? What did you see?"

"I didn't see Rosalie this time. Just Bette and her mother. Let me tell you—Bette's mom wasn't very nice. I mean, she really was hard on her. Physically abusive and threatening."

Detra Ann rubbed her thin shoulders. "I never knew."

"Yep, I encountered the old bat the other day, and she just showed up in this vision too. Evil woman." I probably shouldn't have said it like that, judging by the frown on Detra Ann's face, but it was the truth. Mrs. Hollingsworth was an old bat and horrible, like the Wicked Witch of the West. I couldn't believe the way she talked to Bette; it really got under my skin.

"What happened?" Detra Ann asked. "Did you find out what Rosalie had to tell her?"

I couldn't hide my disappointment from her. "Not exactly. But I think Bette's mother was as friendly as a rabid cat. She practically threatened Rosalie. I don't know. The vision was brief, too brief to get much."

Detra Ann looked confused. "Why would she threaten Rosalie? Because of her claims? Was she really Bette's sister?"

I hesitated. "I don't know yet. I'm going to keep trying, though. When I'm not working, of course."

"You really think Bette's mother abused her?"

"Yes, she slapped her to the ground because she allowed Rosalie in the house. Seems kind of harsh to blame the kids for what the parents did."

"Wow, Nancy Drew. Okay. Well, I'll ask around and see if anyone knows what happened to Rosalie; maybe Bette mentioned her to someone at the historical society? They've known her longer than I have. Someone knows something." Detra Ann turned off the light and headed for the staircase. Guess that was our cue to leave. "And if that doesn't work, I can talk to Carrie Jo. She loved Bette like a second mother."

"I'm not giving up. I'll try to tap in again and see if I can find out anything else. It just takes a lot out of me, and I have to keep my psychometry here at the shop. There's trouble on the home front. It's a long story, but let's just say I'm in hot water with the sibling."

"Oh," Detra Ann said with a laugh, "I'd prefer you keep the antiques here, anyway. Not that I don't trust you, but anything can happen. I wouldn't want a tragedy on your shoulders."

"That works for me, Boss Lady. I don't need that kind of pressure."

"It's Detra Ann, Aggie." She wasn't giving an inch on the nickname. "You have no idea how dangerous dabbling with all this stuff can be. I could tell you stories that would make your hair curl. Well, this is enough for now. I need time to think, and we've got customers today. Let's go take care of the living, shall we?"

"What kind of stories?" I wanted to ask, but I never would. She would tell me if she wanted me to know, and sometimes things were better left unsaid. All I knew was that we still had a lot to uncover about poor Bette Hollingsworth.

A small shadow, about the size of a cat, caught my attention in my peripheral vision. Then it skittered away into one of the back rooms. Odd. Detra Ann hadn't noticed it, and I decided that it was my mind playing tricks on me again. Devecheaux Antiques had too many shadows to keep track of, and it seemed like they were multiplying daily. Despite all of that, I liked this apartment. I liked the feel of it. If it did turn out that I could rent it, I would definitely be interested. I had student loan money and a small paycheck from the Devecheauxs. Maybe I could manage.

Detra Ann glanced at me. Oh, dear. She saw the shadow cat too? I smiled and pretended nothing had happened. "We better get down there, or Henri will have our hides," I said as I hurried down the steps ahead of her.

I blocked it all out of my mind. Kind of. That was one less strange thing for me to deal with at the moment, and whatever that shadow thing was would just have to wait.

Besides, if I wanted to move into this apartment and finally have some freedom, I would have to learn to live with the spirits.

*This should be interesting...*

## *Chapter Twelve—Bette*

"Rosalie, what is it? What do you see? You have to tell me, sister." I touched her hand hoping to comfort her, but a strange chill came over me. A chill that seeped into my bones and threatened to sicken me. I could not account for the phenomenon at all. I withdrew my hand quickly.

With trembling fingers, Rosalie turned the cup around in her hands, viewing the contents from different angles. We were taking a real risk having her come back here again after what happened with Mother last time. But there was more she had seen in the tea leaves that stormy night, and I just had to know. After a few moments of silence, Rosalie's dark, dreamy eyes finally met mine. They were wet with unshed tears. Despite her sad expression, she said in a low voice, "Fear not in this teacup, for good fortune more than outweighs the bad." Her voice sounded robotic, the wording practiced. Rosalie looked past me, as if I weren't even there. What strangeness was this? Was this some sort of trickery? I couldn't believe that. Why would she want to keep the tea leaves from me?

"Rosalie?"

"I see a marriage, a happy marriage, possibly yours or a friend's. It seems certain that this good fortune will be most unexpected, and it will forever change your life." Rosalie put the cup back on the saucer and wiped at her eyes and then closed them. She took a deep breath, and her gaze met mine. Such pain, such heartbreak. Was it about me?

"Rosalie? You aren't telling me the truth, are you? What did you really see in my cup? Don't hold anything back, please. I must know. Will we forever be friends? Rosalie? Speak the truth."

"I should never have come to Hollingsworth Manor. And I definitely shouldn't have returned. I thought...I don't know why I came here at all except I had to know for sure. I thought you knew about me and that, like your mother, you hated me. I thought you knew and blamed me for all of it. My mother's obsession with your father and his fortune ruined our lives, and here I am continuing in her footsteps. I truly want nothing from you, Bette. Only to be your sister. Forgive me." Rosalie rose from the table as the lights came on. It was not storming tonight, except for the one that now churned in my heart.

For a moment, I thought I heard footsteps, the sounds of high heels clicking down the downstairs hallway, but it was nothing. Jennifer, our housekeeper and Mother's creature, had taken the night off, thankfully. I never liked the woman. She had a habit of spying on me and telling all my secrets.

"Rosalie, there is nothing to forgive. I am surprised by what you've told me, but I believe you. I certainly do not blame you, and neither should you blame yourself. My father was practically a stranger to me. I have no ill feelings toward him or you. Surely you must be wrong about your mother. I have not seen her or heard anything about her. If my mother knew, she certainly did not tell me anything. Don't leave, Rosalie."

To my surprise, the dark-haired beauty sat back down, but she did not appear quite as comfortable or as confident as before. She was truly troubled, and I had to know why. What had changed? She must have recognized a bad omen in my tea leaves. I had to know what that omen meant.

"I don't know what to say," Rosalie confessed as she tugged a pale blue handkerchief from her tasseled purse. She dabbed at her nose and eyes.

"There is nothing to say—just tell me the truth. There is certainly no need to apologize. For what, being born? Let us tell only the truth to one another. That is all that needs to be spoken between us. We can't change what's happened, but we can be honest with one another. We are not our mothers. Tell me what you saw, Rosalie. Please, tell me."

"Very well," she answered as she eased back into place. "That is what I came back here for, anyway. I wanted to leave you with something, a gift from me to you. But this was not the gift I wished to bestow. I do not want to tell you what I saw or what it means because it is the worst possible symbol—it is a snake, Bette. A coiled snake. It means deception and death, and it will spring suddenly upon you without warning."

"What?" I asked breathlessly. I could not believe my ears. I knew it would be bad, but this I was not prepared to hear at all. "Am I going to die? That is what you are saying, isn't it? I will die a sudden death?"

Rosalie shook the cup again and stared at the leaves. "It is not clear. Do not ask me anything else, please. I did not come to be a doomsayer but to share my gift with you before I leave. Please, I should go."

I rose to argue with her when I heard the front door opening. That familiar jingle of my mother's key ring alarmed me. Had she returned home early from her conference? This was not like her at all. She normally milked every moment she could from those sales gatherings. She fancied herself quite the saleswoman even though we had an entire room dedicated to storing boxes of skin cream and makeup.

"Oh no! It's my mother," I whispered to Rosalie, who sprang to her feet in fear. She snatched her purse off the table and held it for dear life. "You have to go, Rosalie. Out the back door. Go through the dining room door, and don't let her see you. Please, you have to go!"

"How will you explain this, Bette?" She pointed at the teapot and cups.

"Leave that to me. You have to go! She can't find you here!"

I practically shoved her out of the kitchen as I raced back to the breakfast table. If I hid one of the cups, it wouldn't appear suspicious. That's what I would do! Hide one of the cups! I reached for the cup and saw that it had been chipped. That must have happened the last time Mother surprised us during the reading. It was just a small chip, but Mother would certainly notice it.

"Bette? Why are all the lights on? Who is that running down the hall?"

I wasn't prepared to answer any of Mother's questions. She stared at me; it was a hard stare that melted my soul. Yes, I could feel myself shrinking inch by inch. And in a matter of seconds, she knew the truth. She knew it all. Her eyes went to the table and then to me.

In less than five seconds, she cleared the distance between us and slapped me to the ground.

## *Chapter Thirteen—Aggie*

I tried to take my mind off the shop and everything else that was going on up there by thumbing through my art history book from college. I was excited to start school, but I wasn't happy about going part-time. I would miss Detra Ann and Henri—they were like extended family already. I really loved working for them.

Picking out my courses for the semester wasn't hard at all. Art history and cultural anthropology were on the top of the list, and then all the other required courses fell behind.

It would be the first time in history that I wouldn't have to live in my perfect sister's shadow. It also meant that I wouldn't have her to depend on to cover me when I screwed up. Not quite sure how I felt about that.

Detra Ann had given me a few days off to get ready for school. I needed it. All of this chasing after spirits and visions was wearing me out.

Bette and Rosalie were still on my mind, but I had other things I needed to get done. Whatever was hidden in their past would have to stay there for now. I hadn't seen Patrice, and we really were not speaking to each other at the moment. She had avoided me like the plague since she found out that her weird sister was even more out there than she thought.

It was hurtful, but I was used to it. This was her pattern with me. She shut me out a lot while we were in high school. None of her friends would want to hang out with me, and she was just too popular. The beautiful Patrice, perfect in every way. I was the complete opposite, the oddball and way too artsy for her snobby friends.

Even strangers would walk up to her and tell her how beautiful she was. I don't know how many times we were stopped and she was told, "Wow, you could be a model." Then they'd turn to me and say, "Y'all look nothing alike."

Self-esteem out the window.

Patrice had a good heart, and I knew she loved me. She just didn't know how to handle my awkwardness. Heck, I didn't know how to handle it either. Okay, so maybe focusing on the present wasn't the best idea.

I started to think about Rosalie again and what she had to tell Bette. Did she ever get to talk to Bette again? It's true, sometimes things just go unsaid. It would be nice to have someone to talk to about this. There was so much I wanted to share with Patrice. I guess we'd never have that kind of relationship.

A familiar scent started to fill the room. *Surely it can't be what I think it is. I don't even have the tea set with me. No cup, no saucer. Nothing.* I had to be losing my mind. The knock on my door took me out of my thoughts. "Come in," I said, happy for the interruption.

"Aggie? Mom's been calling you for fifteen minutes," Patrice said, walking into my room.

I was surprised but thankful. "Really? Sorry, I must have been daydreaming. What does she want, Patrice?" I eased off the bed and stretched. Man, I was tired.

"I could tell you, but where's the fun in that? Just be warned—she's on the warpath."

I stomped my foot like a child. "That's all you can tell me? Thanks, Patrice. You're a big help."

"I do what I can," she said as she smirked at me and turned to walk downstairs. She stopped at my door, turning slowly around to look back at me.

"What is it?" I asked.

"I just wanted to say that..." She paused for a moment and started sniffing around.

"Yeah, go ahead. What did you want to say?" Now she was acting weird. I was usually the only one who sniffed the air like a bloodhound.

"Are you smoking in here?" Patrice asked me suspiciously.

"You know I don't smoke. What is wrong with you?" I was confused at the accusation. Was she trying to get me grounded for life? I mean, come on. I've never even tried a cigarette. Did she just come in here to lay something else on my plate?

"Nothing," she replied, walking around my room with her perfect little nose up in the air.

"What are you doing?" I asked.

"It's nothing, I'm just...it smells like..."

"It smells like what?" I shot back.

"I'm not sure, but it's something that I've smelled before. Are you sure that you aren't smoking in here? You know Mom and Dad would not be happy."

"Patrice, I'm not smoking in here or anywhere else. Maybe you're smoking wacky weed. You know I'm supposed to be the weird one, not you. Now what did you want to tell me?"

*Ugh. I can't wait to move out!*

"I just wanted to say that I'm sorry for avoiding you. I don't know how to deal with stuff that doesn't make sense. It's easier for me to just avoid it," Patrice said with a sad smile. She sat down next to me and started to flip through my cultural anthropology book.

"Apology accepted. It's not easy for me either, you know."

Patrice thumbed through the book. "I know. So, this is what you are studying this semester?"

"Yes, why? Is there something wrong with that?" I knew this was her way of changing the subject. She always did this when we were making up. It was her way of saying she was sorry and we should move on.

"No, no. It's just different, but that's you. You're *different*," she replied with a laugh.

"Yes, I know. It's pretty interesting, you know. Different cultures and their beliefs. Maybe you should go outside of your little bubble every once in a while."

Patrice did live within her own little bubble. She'd had the same friends since elementary school and didn't really have any interest in making new ones. They were all kind of those cheerleader types. I think one of them was even an Azalea Trail Maid. You know, smart, pretty and just well-rounded. None of them liked me. I hung out with the band geeks and chess club sort of people. Smart but introverted.

"So, have you had any more of your so-called visions?"

"Are you sure you want to know?" I asked suspiciously.

"Not really."

"I didn't think so."

Patrice began to sniff the air again. "Do you smell that? It's that same scent again. I know I've smelled it before. I just can't put my finger on it."

"Is Mom cooking supper? I guess I better go face the music."

"No, not yet. Oh well, maybe it's your perfume or just your overall funkiness," she sassed as she got up from the bed, rubbing the top of my head. I hated it when she did that.

"Yeah, okay. Thanks."

She shut the door, and I forgot all about going to see Mom. I flopped back on the bed and went back to daydreaming about Bette and Rosalie. They seemed so close, like best friends even though they didn't really know one another. I wished I could find out more. Hopefully, Detra Ann had some news for us. If I could only see or talk with spirits more frequently. My ability seemed to be limited to visions through touch.

Just then, Patrice flung open my door. *Great, we're back to not knocking. Well, it was good while it lasted.*

"What do you need now?"

"Nothing, I just remembered where I've smelled that scent before." Her lovely eyes were wide and her cheeks slightly flushed.

"Oh, goody. And where might that be?"

"Grandma!" Patrice replied, smiling and shutting the door before I could say anything.

*Gosh she's irritating. Grandma? And she thinks I'm strange? Does she think my room smells like an old lady?*

Wait! No, that couldn't be possible. I mean, that would mean she was like me, and that was out of the question. There's no way, right? Could Patrice smell the clove scent too?

I tripped on my own feet going after Patrice. "Wait a minute! Do you smell clove?" I asked breathlessly.

"Hmm... Yes, that's it." Patrice tilted her head.

"Are you sure?"

"Why are you asking me like that?" she replied, and then her face went pale. She knew *exactly* why I was asking her.

"I think you know why. You can smell her too!" I exclaimed through gritted teeth, "How could you keep this from me?"

Patrice frowned and glanced over her shoulder. "Keep your voice down. What are you talking about?"

"You smell things, don't you? Do you see things too?" I pressed without mercy.

"Every once in a while, but who doesn't have certain familiar scents pop up? It's not weird. I'm not weird. And will you keep your voice down?"

"The fact that you are smelling clove cigarette smoke *is* a little strange," I huffed.

"How so? For all I know, it's on you, your hair, your clothes." Patrice glared at me with her slender arms crossed. Did she really have no clue?

"You know that cup and saucer I brought home?"

"Yeah? What about them?" she shot back.

I leaned in closer to her. "Clove has been very significant within my visions, and there is a strong connection to the people who owned that tea set."

Patrice looked like a deer caught in headlights, her big green eyes wide. If she didn't know before, she definitely knew why I was asking now. She had abilities too. My sister, the normal, perfect child, was actually an oddball like me. At least to some degree.

"You don't think that I..."

"Welcome to the Oddball Club, dear sister."

"This can't be happening," Patrice mumbled. "The only explanation is that you've been smoking. And I'm not the only one who thinks so. I've got news for you. Mom thinks you've been smoking too." Patrice wasn't happy at all about her current predicament.

"I'm not smoking, crazy. But I could use your help, Trice."

"Help?" Patrice asked. "With what?"

I smiled sheepishly. "Maybe with both of us, we can find out what happened to one of the spirits I've been in contact with lately. I can't seem to ever get a complete message."

"What? No. Aggie, I don't know how this all works, I mean, I just smell things once in a while. I've not experienced anything else."

"Are you sure?" Why didn't I believe her?

"Pretty sure," Patrice replied.

"Ever had any dreams that seemed like they were real?"

Her face lost color again. "Sometimes, but doesn't everyone?" she asked slowly.

"No, Patrice. Not everyone has lucid dreams. Here's another question, have you ever felt like someone was in the room with you, but no one was there? No one you can see."

Patrice sagged slightly and nodded.

"Spirits are all around us, Patrice. They've been trying to connect with you, apparently, and you've been shutting them out. Don't you see? We have gifts that can help people. We just have to learn to use them correctly."

"I don't know. I think you're making a mountain out of a molehill." Patrice shifted on her feet. "This is all too much for me."

"I get that you're afraid, but we can help these spirits. There's something that they've been trying to tell me. I think one of the sisters was hurt by someone and wants her story told. They need me."

"Sisters?" Patrice whispered incredulously.

"Yes. Sisters." I nodded. "Remember what you used to tell me? Sisters forever?"

"Of course I remember. I guess I can't say no to that. What do we need to do?"

I couldn't believe Patrice was willing to help. I hugged her without thinking about it. She did not pull away from me. "We need to go to the shop and make a connection there. I had the clearest vision at the shop. The spirits seem to be able to communicate from that location. Just a little side note, weird stuff happens there, so just be prepared."

"Noted."

I chewed my nail as I thought about how to do this. I wasn't supposed to show up for work for a few more days. I'd taken off for college prep, but this couldn't wait. "I know what to do. I'll let Detra Ann know that I'm bringing my sister to look at the apartment before I sign the lease and to leave it unlocked for us."

"What? You didn't tell me you were moving out. When did you decide this?" Patrice couldn't hide her surprise.

"It just kinda happened." I hurried back to my room to put my shoes on. She trailed after me. "It's just an idea. It's not like I'm moving out of the country. I'll be right down the street."

"I know, it's just I wasn't expecting it. That's all." Patrice crossed her arms and shook her head.

I grabbed her hand and said, "You can come visit me anytime. You'll love it. It's a cute apartment, and I'll need your help decorating."

She perked up. "You'd let me decorate? Are you sure about that?"

I laughed. "I said you can *help* decorate, not do the whole thing."

We were finally getting along. I hoped it would last. What other abilities had Patrice been hiding from me? I could only hope that she and I would find out more about what happened to poor Rosalie.

*Sisters forever…we're coming, Rosalie and Bette! We're coming!*

## Chapter Fourteen—Aggie

The apartment door clicked open, and the air was still and quiet. Our footsteps were the only noise as we walked over the threshold. A cool breeze passed by us, stopping us both in our tracks. "That was weird," Patrice whispered as she touched my elbow. "But it is nice in here. I like it."

"Yeah, it's a nice apartment. It has two bedrooms and one bath. Like I said, weird things happen on this property." I shut the door behind us.

"Seriously. Are you sure you would want me to move in here? Imagine Mom's face when she finds out we're both leaving." Patrice grabbed my arm and pushed in closer to me.

"I'm not even sure I am moving in. But it makes sense for someone like me to move into a place like this. Doesn't it?"

Patrice let out a halfhearted "I guess so." We moved over to the table where the missing cup and saucer had been set out. It was nice of Detra Ann to put them back up here—it felt good to know she trusted me. Yes, this setup seemed almost like an invitation.

"What do we do now?" Patrice asked as she studied the cup.

"We wait, but I think we both should hold the cup and saucer."

"Wait? Wait for what? No way," Patrice whispered. "This is all just too weird."

With a patient smile, I said, "We are on a ghost hunt, Patrice. We have to wait for the ghosts to show up." My sister was something else. Turning up her perfect little nose at me.

"It's too nerve-racking to just sit here. I'm not doing that, Aggie; I don't care what you say. You know I'm a take-action kind of gal. I have to do something, not sit around and wait for the ghosts to appear. That's just not me."

"Fine. I'm learning too, you know. Let's try something else. What do you have in mind?" We sat across from each other, and neither of us spoke a word for a few minutes. Despite her need for action, Patrice had no ideas either. I tapped my finger on the table, trying to come up with a plan we could implement.

"A seance, maybe?" Patrice asked hesitantly.

"Really?" I shot back. "You want to try holding a seance?"

"I don't know," Patrice said as she crossed her arms. "Do you have a better idea?" Footsteps coming toward us stopped her mid-sentence. I did not move, and I could hear Patrice's breath quicken. The odd shuffling noise stopped, and we both stood up slowly from the table, bracing for God-knows-what.

A shadow passed through the doorway leading out from the kitchen, causing us both to gasp. "What was that?" Patrice stuttered as she reached for me. "Was that a ghost? I mean, a real ghost?"

*A Cup of Shadows*

"I don't know, Patrice. Let's not assume anything."

We moved toward the doorway, and the shadow passed in front of us again. This time I could make out the shape. It wasn't the small, cat-shaped shadow that I had seen before. The shadow was much larger, closer to our size. Before we could pursue it, I heard a strange sound. The cup and saucer on the table began to clank together.

"Aggie!" Patrice called out frantically.

"Bette?" I clutched her hand and called out.

"What are you doing?" Patrice said, her voice shaky.

"Grab my phone."

"Why?"

"Just do it," I shouted back.

Patrice grabbed my phone and handed it to me. I hit the voice memo app and began to record. My fingers were shaking and my heart was pounding, but at least I wasn't by myself.

"Bette? If you're here, give us a sign." I waited a few seconds and played the audio back. "Oh my God!" There was a crackling sound on my phone.

*Don't freak out, Aggie. This is what you came here for. This is what you asked for.* "If that's you, Bette, I need to know what message you have for us. I am Detra Ann's friend. Please talk to us."

Again, a crackling sound came through like a bad radio reception. Only this time I hadn't hit the stop button. I wasn't listening to a recording. This was live and in person.

"What do we need to know about the tea set?" More noise. "Please tell me." I let the recorder go for a few minutes longer, then stopped it and then hit the play button. My voice played back, *"Bette?"*

*Yes...*

"I heard something!" Patrice shrieked beside me.

"Shhhh, let's keep listening." I waved my hand at her.

"If that's you, Bette, I need to know what message you have for us. I am Detra Ann's friend. Please talk to us."

Again, another faint response. *Yes, message...*

My voice cut in again, "What do we need to know about the tea set?"

*"Find Rosalie,"* the sweet, familiar voice whispered.

The recording continued, "Please tell me."

Bette's spirit responded slowly, *"Tell Carrie Jo to find Rosalie."*

"Rosalie? What happened to her? Who's Carrie Jo?" Patrice whispered fearfully.

"Carrie Jo is a friend of Detra Ann and Bette's. She's a dream catcher," I whispered back.

"I don't understand what that means," Patrice responded, sounding frustrated.

"Rosalie told Bette she had to leave Mobile because someone wanted to hurt her. I'm guessing she was murdered but needs us to find out who did it. That's why she's been trying to connect to us. I have my suspicions about who would want to hurt Rosalie."

"Who do you think it is?"

"I think Bette's own mother had something to do with it, but I have no way to prove that one way or the other. Not in a legal sense. I can't go to the police with visions or EVPs."

Patrice pursed her lips. "That's true. So, now what do we do?"

The only thing we could do—we had to tell Detra Ann. "I will find the Boss Lady and let her listen to this message. Hopefully she will know what to do to help Bette. She was supposed to ask around and see if anyone knew anything about Rosalie. I'm sure she will be interested to know that Bette asked for Carrie Jo. Like I said, Carrie Jo has some sort of ability. I'm guessing she might be able to find out more info for us."

"Is everyone in this town some sort of wacko?" Patrice huffed.

"You're a wacko too, so I wouldn't say too much about it."

She groaned. "Don't remind me."

Hopefully we could get closer to the truth now. This town was so tight-lipped. If anyone did know anything about Rosalie, they probably had already passed on by now. Everything else would just be considered a rumor or idle gossip.

But Bette's spirit was restless, and she was reaching out for help. This teacup had been the trigger, the thing she needed to make contact. It saddened me to know that she'd had to wait so long for me to show up.

*Please, God. Let me help her.*

I just couldn't get the question out of my mind: What happened to Rosalie?

"Okay, Patrice. We're going to do this my way. I have to hold the cup. Let's do this together. This EVP isn't enough to present to Detra Ann. Help me, Patrice. Please, for once, just trust me and help me."

I sat at the table and held the cup in my hand. I waited for her answer. To my surprise, she didn't put up a fight. No argument, no "better idea." She sat across from me without a word. With a nod, she reached her hand out and touched the cup.

*Sisters forever...*

## Chapter Fifteen—Bette

Skipping school was a new experience for me. It was wildly freeing but also terrifying. I hadn't been much of a rule-breaker thus far in my life, but surprisingly I liked the fear. No doubt I'd be found out—my mother had this town wired, as they say—but I had to take a chance. Time was not on my side. I had no idea when Rosalie would leave Mobile, but she hadn't been in school at all this week. I hadn't been given a chance to offer a proper goodbye.

My Greenfire bicycle with the shimmery blue tassels glided down Herbert Street. Maybe I would go to school after my time with Rosalie. I was never tardy and rarely absent. Surely Mr. White, our principal, wouldn't make a big deal over it. Hopefully he would not call my mother and rat me out.

*Too late now, Bette. Too late to worry about any of that.*

Just as Debbie told me, Herbert Street dead-ended on a sandy dirt road. I hated riding my bicycle on sand—I was notoriously clumsy, anyway, whether sand or pavement or sidewalk. I paused momentarily to peek ahead, but I didn't spot any houses. Debbie said that Rosalie lived in a small white house; she'd come by her place a few times to sell eggs for her Papa. She didn't have much else to say about Rosalie except that they always bought eggs.

I didn't like that I couldn't see past the hedges that lined the elusive pathway, but I scolded myself for being a fraidy cat. I had no time to waste being timid. With some effort, I rode the Greenfire across the sand. The front tire wobbled a bit, but I managed to make it past the curve. Then the path widened a bit, opening up to a small clearing with a tidy cottage in the center of it. It looked like something out of a fairy tale. White cookie-cutter blinds, a neat porch with a rocking chair positioned next to a small round table. It was incredibly small compared to Hollingsworth Manor, but I imagined it was full of love. Bright and sunny with lots of love. Why would Rosalie want to leave this place? Maybe she had no choice. That's what it sounded like. Like she couldn't afford to stay. Did she have no relatives at all? As I dismounted my bicycle, I peered up into the trees. Sunlight scattered down from the leaves overhead. In that moment, all the cheeriness of the day vanished. A cold breeze fluttered past me, kicking up leaves around my feet.

Why was I thinking of Hansel and Gretel? Why did that comparison terrify me?

*Come on, Bette. There's nothing to be afraid of here.* No, this was a lovely place to live. Why did Rosalie have to leave when we'd just found one another? I wondered how long she knew I was her sister...certainly longer than I'd known about her. I propped the bike up under the hickory tree since my kickstand did not want to work properly. It got stuck sometimes. I'd been meaning to oil the hinge but just hadn't gotten around to it.

I took a step onto the cleanly swept porch and saw a tidy flower garden. There were lots of whimsical touches too, like a mermaid statue in a circular rock garden beside the house. Lots of interesting things to see, even a blue bottle tree, the kind that traps unwanted spirits. I only knew that because Mother's previous housekeeper, Iola, knew all about those sorts of things, spirits and whatnot. I missed her. Even though she never hugged me, I liked to imagine that she cared about bony, awkward me. Like Rosalie, I had no real family beyond my mother. No one to depend on for my livelihood.

I decided not to waste another minute since we probably didn't have much time together. No sense dawdling in the yard. What a wonderful door—a half door. *Another reason to think of Hansel and Gretel. Yes, it's like a place straight from a storybook.*

"Rosalie?" I called softly as I climbed the steps and peeked inside the top half of the open door. The inside of Rosalie's home was just as magical, from what I could see. There was a lumpy yet comfortable-looking sofa covered in a bright-colored crocheted blanket. Next to it was a neat stack of magazines. I heard soft humming from a room just beyond my view. "Rosalie?"

The humming ceased and soft footsteps came my way. "Bette?" Rosalie's surprised yet happy expression filled my heart with joy. "I thought you were Byron, but I am glad to see you. Come inside, Bette!"

"I hope you don't mind me stopping by unannounced. I don't know your phone number," I said apologetically. "Byron? Do I know him? Is he helping you move?"

"Yes, you know him, silly goose. He went to school with us, Byron Maybury. I am going to marry him. At least I am thinking about marrying him." She appeared joyful, bubbling about the future, but I didn't feel joy. All I could sense was sadness. Sadness at losing my only sister. Rosalie hugged me, and I enjoyed the wonderful scent of my sister. She smelled like tea and rosemary and something else. Something I couldn't put my finger on but would always remember. Even after she was gone.

Gone.

I shivered at the word that popped into my mind unbidden.

"You never have to announce yourself, and I don't have a phone anymore. It's a good thing you came when you did. I am leaving tonight with Byron. He's going to basic training—he joined the Army—and we have to drive a long ways. All the way to South Dakota. I have never been to South Dakota, have you?"

"South Dakota?" I grabbed her hands and pleaded with her. "Surely you can wait a little bit. Don't leave yet. Why so soon, Rosalie? We are just getting to know one another. I don't want our friendship to come to an end—surely Byron would understand. Can't I meet him, at least? Why do you have to leave? Do you need money? Is that why you are leaving?" I blabbered on, hoping to convince her of how desperate I felt.

Rosalie shook her dark head. "Byron has to leave, and I am going with him. The bank owns the cottage, since my mother owed a lot of money, but I have a future with Byron. I told you I wanted to travel. Well, this is how I do it."

I couldn't believe my ears. "You haven't been in school this week and I thought maybe my mother said something to you but you're getting married? Is that what you're saying?"

Rosalie flashed her brilliant smile. I'd never seen anyone wear wine-colored lipstick. Not in person. Only in the movies. She did seem like a movie star. A glamorous, feisty movie star. "Yes, I think I am. He must be the one. His timing is impeccable, don't you think?"

"You think? Shouldn't you know for sure? This seems so sudden. It all feels like a crazy dream, Rosalie."

"More like a crazy roller coaster ride."

"I didn't even know you were engaged. Are you sure this isn't my mother's doing? She can be quite pushy, and she's determined to dislike you, but that shouldn't bother you. Mother doesn't like me either, and I am her own daughter. She cannot stop us from being sisters." I rambled on in a rush. I wanted Rosalie to know that I needed her. That I wanted to get to know her. I didn't want her to leave so soon. We had to stay in touch. We had to stay connected in some way. How would I get to know her if she was in another state? Or God knows where.

*Gone. She'll be gone...*

Rosalie chattered on like she didn't hear the whisper, but I heard it. I know I heard it. "Byron is in the military now, Bette. He's my boyfriend. We're getting married as soon as we get to his first duty station. He isn't the most handsome guy, or the smartest, to be honest, but he has a good heart. He graduated from our school last year. He's so wonderful. I wish you could get to know him. You do remember him, don't you? I think I love him, Bette." Rosalie sat on the couch and took my hands, pulling me to sit down with her.

"I don't understand why you have to leave. I wish with all my heart I had known about you before. How could I have not known about you? Tell me the truth—it's my mother, isn't it? She's forcing you to leave Mobile." Tears brimmed in my eyes. I believed that Mother was the cause of all this. I believed that with all my soul. I didn't need my sister to confirm that fear, yet I guess I wanted to hear that I was right.

"Listen to me, Bette Hollingsworth. We are sisters forever. No one can take that away from us. No matter how much time or space passes between us, we will always be sisters. Our mothers wasted their lives fighting over our father. My mother believed that she deserved a portion of his fortune, but I don't want anything. I can't say what is right and what is wrong, but I want more from life than hiding my face and feeling ashamed for breathing air. I know what people say about me."

"I never heard any gossip about you, Rosalie," I lied in hopes that she would feel at ease and change her mind.

"It's okay, Bette. You did not create this storm any more than I did. It is not our fight. If I stay, Mrs. Hollingsworth will make it her life's work to divide us. Please understand, all I want is to find my own way. If that means moving away, then so be it. You must agree with me. You are no stranger to your mother, and my mother was no match for her. Not that Mama was innocent; I mean...we all know how I got here."

I dabbed away my tears and continued to plead with her, "Rosalie, you are here and that is all that matters. My father must have loved your mother."

"Not so much, I think. Look around, Bette. We have lost everything, and we didn't have much to begin with."

"No! They loved each other. You are the proof of that love. If you think this is what you need to do, I support you. I won't lie and say that it doesn't grieve me, but I understand, Rosalie. We must always stay in touch. All through your adventures, we must always stay connected—promise me that."

In her soft musical voice, she said, "I promise and swear."

"And if you get in a pinch, if you need something. If things with Byron don't work out—"

Rosalie's confidence vanished just like that. "Don't say that, Bette. You'll jinx me."

Rosalie wasn't as certain about her relationship with Byron as she first intimated. That worried me. What was happening here? This was like something out of a novel I read! I didn't know what to do.

All I could say was, "Please, tell me how I can help you. Let me help. There has to be something I can do."

Rosalie's eyes flashed. "Mother. You can help me connect with my mother."

I hadn't expected that answer. "I don't know how to do that, Rosalie. I wouldn't know the first thing about it."

"I'll show you," she whispered desperately as she grabbed my hands again. I was terrified, but I listened to her hopeful plea with a willing heart. "Everyone has a kind of energy, Bette. You are my sister, and I know you have the same kind of energy as I do. I can feel it surging through your veins. If you could lend that energy to me, a connection can be made. Yes! I should have thought of this before. I can't connect on my own. Believe me, I've tried. My grief...it prevents me. Do this one thing for me, and I will never ask you for anything else. I promise, sister."

Still unsure what this meant, I glumly agreed. I was certain to disappoint her, but I was willing to try. *Whatever I can do. That's what I said.* I had to be a woman of my word, and she was after all my sister. Without saying another word, Rosalie left me on the couch and returned in a few minutes with a teapot and cup set. The brew smelled spicy, like Rosalie's unique perfume.

She lit a clove cigarette, took a few puffs and put the tea tray on the steamer trunk she was using as a coffee table. As she poured the hot water over the tea leaves, I watched anxiously. I couldn't account for the sudden butterflies I felt in my stomach, but there was no denying that they were there.

*What do I do? What can I do?*

Rosalie handed me the cup and asked me to take a sip. "Take small sips and look deep. Look and tell me what you see, sister."

Obediently, I sipped the sour brew and stared into the dregs of the cup. "Tea leaves, Rosalie. That is all I see. I am sorry. I knew I would disappoint you. What should I be looking for?" I asked, hoping for further instructions.

"Shadows. Look for the shadows, sister. They are there, swirling in your cup. Take a deep breath and see. You are holding a cup of shadows." Her voice sounded kind of sing-songy and lyrical. She continued to whisper instructions, but I wasn't seeing anything. Not at first.

I gasped at the sight of the swirling shadows I held within the teacup. Wait! I knew this cup. This was my mother's china. How did it end up here? I thought about the question, but I couldn't form it in my mouth because something else was happening.

I was saying something, whispering, but it wasn't my voice. I fought against it, but there was no denying it. I wasn't myself. I was someone else. My lips were numb, and my throat tingled. It was a strange, disconcerting sensation. And then I heard her voice. It came from my lips.

Dark and husky and full of pain. Camellia! This had to be Rosalie's mother!

*Rosalie...*

"Mother? It is you! Give me the cup, Bette. Let me see. Don't struggle, sister. Don't be afraid."

I wished I could speak to her, but I could do nothing except stare into the cup. Even as the cup left my hands, I saw nothing but the swirling shadows. I could feel Rosalie's cool skin on mine briefly. The shadows twisted and moved and became something more solid. I could almost see a face emerge, a dark, shadowy face.

"Mother?" Rosalie asked hopefully. I could hear her, but I couldn't see her. At least my lips had stopped tingling. I was beginning to feel I had control over my body again. But I needed to let go, didn't I? I had to let go and let her speak. I tried to relax, and my body sagged against the back of the couch.

*No, this isn't right! I can't do this!*

I tried to protest, but only a strange gurgling sound came out.

*Rosalie...gone...*

"I know you're gone, Mother. I miss you. Can you tell me who hurt you? Who did it? Who killed you?"

Her mother was killed? What? My mind flooded with images of a woman who looked very much like Rosalie only taller. Yes, tall and willowy.

Camellia...she hadn't seen her. She hadn't heard her.

I knew what she would say. I knew who it was even though I never saw her face.

Camellia had been in her garden, her hat tucked down over her eyes. She hadn't seen the car pull up. Hadn't realized she was being watched as she worked in the thyme and mint. Not until the footsteps shuffled up behind. Camellia recognized the scraping of metal, like from her garden hoe. This was the sound it made as you pulled it out of the ground. She heard the thud and saw the splattering of blood across the white flowers. It stained the impatiens.

As she lay on the ground, her hat cocked off to the side, unable to move or do anything except die, she watched as the two shadows became one. Oh yes, the sun had been shining, but there were a few shadows.

Now she was a shadow.

"Mother, give me a name. Tell us, please."

I wanted no part of this. I sobbed as Camellia grasped my neck. She shook me but not from the outside, from the inside. Her hand was inside of me—she was inside of me. I had never felt such rage, such acute anger!

*It wasn't me! It wasn't me*! I pleaded with the shadow of Camellia. She had no mercy. I thought I would die on that couch. Die next to my sister.

"No! Let her go! Mother!"

At the sound of Rosalie's voice, Camellia released me, but it was too late. My face was on fire, my throat was raw, and the spirit remained close. So very close. Would I ever be rid of it? Rosalie pleaded with me, but I wanted nothing from her. Nothing at all. She knew this would happen! She knew and asked me to step into that world.

"Bette, wait! Please!"

I practically crawled to the front door. I screamed and cried as I staggered down the steps. Rosalie called after me, but those pleas fell on deaf ears. I wanted nothing to do with any of this, now or ever. *Mother, how could you? How could you have killed her?*

Rosalie betrayed me—I felt so betrayed. Everyone used me. Everyone. Even my own sister. I had nothing left. I continued to cry as I pushed my bike down the sandy path. Rosalie chased me for a bit until I turned around briefly and screamed at her.

"No! Don't ask me to do that again!"

Once I cleared the slick sandy patch, I got on my bike and rode hard. But I couldn't go to school. I had to face the evil. I had to tell her what I knew, how I knew it. No, I would never be able to unring the bell, but I wanted her to know that I saw it all. Come what may, I had to confront her. I'd never felt such a storm of emotions. Fear but also anger. Utter disappointment and feelings I couldn't even express.

Tears I knew, though. I knew tears. I'd had a lifetime of tears, and it was only going to get worse.

I cried all the way home.

## *Chapter Sixteen—Aggie*

As the session ended and the vision faded, Patrice cried her eyes out. I knew I would see something, but my sister?

"I can't do this, Aggie. Please. No more."

I didn't know what to say, so I put my arms around her. "It's okay, Patrice. I should never have asked you to do this. I am so sorry."

"She killed her, Aggie. I think she killed her. Did you see what I saw? How is that possible? How is any of this possible? If I didn't see it myself, I wouldn't have believed it. I'm really not cut out for this. I just can't." She hugged me tight.

"Let's go. I'll drive you home," I attempted at comforting her, but my sister was having none of it. She was terrified, and it was all my fault.

"No. I need to think, Aggie. Please, give me a little time to think. I don't think I could live here. Not if this was going to happen again. I can't do it."

I could feel my face flush. I understood exactly what she meant. Just because Patrice had a similar gift as mine didn't mean she was ready to use it. I'd really pushed the envelope with this request. Of course I would back off. I had to. She was my sister.

I couldn't believe it, but I was crying too. All this time, I'd been trying to make Patrice accept me, respect me for who I was, and I hadn't given her the same kindness. She couldn't help being who she was any more than I could. We were sisters, and that meant something to me. This was all wrong. Asking her to do this had been too much too soon. I needed to make this right. If that meant giving her space, then so be it.

"Sure, Patrice. I'm sorry. I'll walk you out, at least. Thanks for trying."

"That sounds great. Please don't mention this to Mom and Dad." Patrice wiped at her eyes with the back of her hand.

"I would never do that, Patty. Never in a million years. I will never betray your trust. This will be our little secret."

Patrice hugged me, and I hugged her back. We had hugged more in the past few minutes than we had in months. Before she released me this time, she whispered in my ear, "Find out what happened to her, Aggie. You have to do that for Bette. She deserves to know. I would go crazy if I lost you. Be careful."

"I promise I will do both. Love you, Patty."

"Love you too. Now stop being sappy and let me go home. I'll run interference for you and tell Mom that you ran by the school. Don't forget to go by and drop off the last of that paperwork before you come home. I don't want to lie to Mom."

With a nod of my head, I promised. We walked down the narrow staircase, the one that led to the back-door exit. I wasn't ready to face Detra Ann yet, but I would have to. This was beyond my expertise. I was going to propose something, something I hoped Detra Ann would agree to.

"Patrice?"

"Yes," she said, turning back toward me.

"I'm truly sorry about how all of this went down. I know it's weird talking to spirits and stuff. I guess I just thought now that we know you have some abilities, maybe we could be like a paranormal dynamic duo or something. Kinda selfish of me, I guess. Are you sure you're okay?"

I really had jumped the gun on this one. Patrice didn't embrace different, out-of-the-box kinds of things like I did. I had been selfish to put this on her.

Patrice sighed. "Aggie, quit worrying about me. I'm okay. I was just a little shaken up, that's all. I'll see you back at home, okay?"

I nodded again and forced a smile. "Okay. See you at home."

Waving to Patrice as she drove away from the shop, I knew that she wasn't alright. I had to give her some closure and make sure I saw this thing through for the both of us now.

I paced, teacup and saucer in hand, waiting for the customer to leave. It felt like an eternity before Detra Ann noticed me.

"Aggie, you are going to wear a hole in the floor pacing back and forth like that," Detra Ann said with a smirk. "Now, what is it you have to tell me?"

She seemed to always know what I was thinking. It was almost uncanny. If I didn't know any better, I would think she was psychic or something.

"I did a little more digging. And by digging, I mean that I spent some more time with this chipped cup," I said, setting the cup down on the counter.

"What did you see this time?"

"I'm more than a little sure that the old bat killed Bette's sister and her sister's mother."

"How?" Detra Ann asked.

"Well, Patrice and I..."

"Patrice?" Detra Ann interrupted.

"Yes, my sister, Patrice."

"Your sister? You told your sister about all of this?"

"Yes, I'm sorry. I know I shouldn't have, but I just found out that she has abilities too and, well, I made a huge mistake."

Detra Ann nodded. "Go on. We will discuss your sister later."

"Fine," I huffed. "Anyway, we made contact with Bette and then decided to see what would happen when we both touched the tea set. Long story short,

Bette said we had to find Rosalie, and she also mentioned Carrie Jo."

"Carrie Jo?"

"Yes, but that's not all," I replied, biting my lip to keep from crying. "Patrice and I both had a vision when we grabbed the cup. It wasn't really clear, but we both saw that Bette and Rosalie found out that Mrs. Hollingsworth killed Rosalie's mother."

"How did they find out?" Detra Ann asked.

I wasn't sure how to even say what I was about to tell her.

"Rosalie and Bette received a message from Camellia, Rosalie's mother."

Detra Ann tilted her head as if the words had gotten a little muffled. "Camellia? But I thought you said she had been murdered."

"Yes, it was a spirit that made the connection. I know it doesn't make sense. I can't make heads or tails of it either. I could be getting all of this wrong. This Carrie Jo? Do you think she can help?"

Detra Ann's eyes filled with tears. "Yes, she would be glad to help Bette. She loved her. You've done more than enough, Aggie. Let's close up shop. If you've got a free minute, you can ride with me to Seven Sisters."

"As much as I would like to, I have to go to the college and drop off paperwork," I reluctantly replied. I really would love to get this all settled and meet Carrie Jo, but I made a promise to Patrice and couldn't let her down. Not now. That would be completely unfair.

"No problem, Aggie. We'll just wait and see what Carrie Jo uncovers. You'll meet her soon enough. She'll need some time, anyway."

"I'm so sorry. I really wanted to get this all figured out for you and Bette and Rosalie. I let you all down." The weight of the world rested on my shoulders. Now *I* felt like crying.

Detra Ann reached out her hand to me. "Aggie, you've just discovered this gift of yours. It's going to take time to perfect it. You'll learn how to use your gift in no time, and this will all be just a faded memory. We all have to go through a learning period with everything we do. You've done a great job, so please don't think that you haven't. I really think you'll like Carrie Jo. Trust me, she has a ton of stories she could tell you."

"I can't wait to meet her. Thanks, Boss Lady."

"You know I don't like that," Detra Ann said as she squeezed my hand, "but this time I'll let it slide."

Driving away from the shop, I couldn't help but think about Bette and Rosalie. I was lucky to have grown up with a sister like Patrice. My moistened cheeks flushed, and anger swelled inside of me at the thought of how their time together had been stolen. If only I could give it back somehow.

My thoughts were interrupted by a soft touch to my cheek and a whisper in my ear...

*Sisters forever.*

## Chapter Seventeen—Aggie

Detra Ann led me into a room that had a name. The Blue Room. I'd never been in a room that had an official name before.

"Carrie Jo, we're here! This is Mary Agnes Kelly, but she prefers Aggie. She is my shop helper. She's the one I was telling you about. Aggie, this is Carrie Jo. I've explained to you how she catches dreams; she visits the past through her dream work. Aggie is similar to you, CJ. Her superpower is touching things. She gets images from touching things, right?"

I laughed nervously. "At times." This scene was too much. The house was too much. Seven Sisters was amazing inside, far larger than I'd imagined walking up the steps. It was like a house-sized time capsule. Hm...I wonder what I would see if I touched those ceramic dogs over there? I ignored the urge and turned my focus to the curly-headed woman with the bright green eyes. There was a little girl around here too, but she didn't join us, only spied from the doorway before running upstairs. I kind of wished she'd come back. I preferred talking to kids than to adults.

"Really? How interesting. Don't let Detra Ann fool you, Aggie. She's got more than one gift, only she likes to pretend she's normal. I guess that's a superpower too. I've not been able to master it." She elbowed her friend playfully and then settled in the chair across from me. Detra Ann shot CJ a go-to-you-know-where look but didn't deny it. "How do you like working at Devecheaux Antiques?" I liked her already. She had an easy way about her. Classy but comfortable. Yep. I stuck out like a sore thumb in my ripped jeans and camo t-shirt. At least there was a unicorn on it. That was kind of cool.

"It's good. Great hours, great people. It's a dream job, really. And I'm not just saying that because my boss is here. I had no idea that teacup would activate me. I spent a lot of time ignoring it. She wouldn't let me." I eyed the familiar set tentatively and was careful not to touch it. I don't think I'd ever forget the look on Bette's face when Camellia took over her body. I guess that's what happened. There was so much I didn't understand about psychometry, but I had every intention of learning all I could.

Detra Ann stood up and said, "Shoot. I have to take this call. I've got to step out, Carrie Jo. Your signal sucks, you know."

"You tell me that every time. We'll be here," Carrie Jo answered as she kicked off her flats and tucked her legs up under her. As modern-looking as she was with her bouncy curls and fitted jeans, she totally fit in here.

I stared around me, just like I used to do when I was a kid and Mom forced me to go to church. That big old cathedral had beautiful statues and glorious stained glass. I never got tired of staring at those amazing features. It had been a long time since I visited church.

"I'll give you a tour after we chat a minute. Thank you for helping Bette. She was such a wonderful woman, so loving, kind to everyone. If it hadn't been for her, I would have starved to death that first month. She did like to cook, and she cooked for me all the time."

"But I didn't help her. Not like I wanted to. I saw her in the cottage...well, Patrice helped me. That's my sister. But I don't know how much I actually helped. I have more questions than answers. I think her mother, Bette's mother, may have had something to do with Camellia's death. Did you see that too?"

Carrie Jo leaned forward and tucked a strand of hair behind her ear. The movement made her seem young and vulnerable and so much like me. "Would you like to see firsthand?"

"How would I do that?" Images of Bette running from Rosalie, of struggling for air and fighting against the murdered woman's spirit, came to mind. I hoped she wasn't suggesting we do something like that.

"Take a walk with me. I'll show you what happened. Thanks to you, I connected to Bette and had a chance to say goodbye. Thanks to you, Aggie. Showing you this will be my way of saying thank you. I would like to help you instill confidence in yourself, Mary Agnes Kelly. You are a rare person. A true gift to the people around you, even if they don't know it yet. They will eventually."

I was breathless. Should I do this? "I'm not sure what you are asking me, Carrie Jo. You make it sound so easy. Just take a walk?"

"Yes, right through that door and into the herb garden. It will be very much like that day, the day she died."

"The day who died?" I asked as I watched Carrie Jo slide her shoes back on. She studied me as if she were asking herself a question: *Is this a good idea? Is she ready?*

I couldn't hear her thoughts, but I was dang good at imagining what people were thinking about me. Yeah, that wasn't a superpower. Carrie Jo's hopeful expression made it impossible for me to say no to her. I wasn't naive like Bette, though. I knew this kind of work put demands on your body, mind and spirit.

"Should we wait for the Boss Lady?"

"It won't take us but a few minutes. We'll probably be gone and back before she comes back. You know how focused Detra Ann can be when it comes to work."

"What do I need to do?"

"Nothing. I'm strong enough to carry us both. You have a natural gift, and not just for psychometry, Aggie. But we don't have to talk about that today."

"Are you going to put me to sleep?"

*A Cup of Shadows*

She laughed, and it was a pretty sound. "No. We'll be wide awake. Or you will be. I'm going to open that door to the garden. You'll take my hand and we'll walk outside together, only we won't go outside. We'll step back into the past, Aggie. Back to Bette's time, back to when she lost Rosalie."

I knew Rosalie was dead, but hearing it, hearing her referred to as "lost" upset me no end. I rose from the chair. I had to see now. I had to see firsthand. If Carrie Jo could help me do that, I would certainly offer her my hand. I had to do this for Bette and for Patrice!

"Okay, I'm ready. What about your daughter? I feel like we should tell someone what we're doing. I don't know why." I laughed nervously as I rose from the comfy chair.

"There's no one here except the three of us. My niece is with her uncle and my son. They've gone to the park."

"Really?" I asked in a surprised voice. "I could have sworn I saw a kid here. Curly hair like yours, bright pink shorts."

"Purple top?" Carrie Jo smiled knowingly.

"Yes! That's right. She went upstairs."

"That's Lily. She's not here. She's like me, Aggie. She dream walks, and she must have known what I intended to do with you. It's complicated. Let's go. I can feel Bette nearby. She's ready to continue our conversation. That's what she always said to me. No matter how long it was since the last time she saw me, she'd say, 'Carrie Jo, let's continue our conversation.' It could have been days, weeks, even months, and she'd pick up right where she left off. I always thought that was kind of magical. One of the things that made her special. Anyway, I'd like you to meet her. Are you ready?"

"I am." I put my hand in Carrie Jo's as she opened the door, and I put my trust in her too. I stepped outside right behind her, just as a warm honey glow surrounded me.

*Oh...how cool. And also a little terrifying.*

*It's okay, Aggie. You don't have to do anything. Just watch.*

But it was too late. I wasn't me. I wasn't watching Bette.

*I was on the pavement, my knee skinned up good. It bled profusely...I'd certainly stain my skirt if I wasn't careful. Oh yes, that was going to leave a stain...*

## *Chapter Eighteen—Bette & Aggie*

I heard the school bell ring, so there was no sense in hurrying. I would have to visit the nurse's station first anyway. This cut would need a bandage. But I deserved it. I deserved this and so much more.

*Rosalie...I am so sorry.*

She was gone, and there was no way to get in touch with her. No address, no phone number. Just stupid Byron Maybury who denied everything. But I knew the truth. I couldn't understand where Rosalie had gone to and why she would leave without Byron. All he would say was he'd changed his mind. He didn't join up and that was it. That was all he had to say about it. It had been a chance meeting anyway. He'd been at Atkins' Gas Station when I arrived with Mother. She went once a week to gas up her sedan.

As she went inside to gossip with Mr. Atkins and pay for the fuel, I spotted Byron and jetted over to him. Byron's shocked expression worried me no end. Did he think no one knew about him and Rosalie? "You know something, Byron Maybury! Tell me what you know!"

He peered over the edge of his glasses at me. "Maybe you should ask her." He nodded toward my mother, who was huffing out of the gas station. She hadn't even noticed I was out of the car. I headed her way quickly and without even looking back.

"What are you doing?" she demanded as I opened the car door.

"I went to the restroom, Mother."

"A public restroom?"

And then I endured a speech about public toilets and restaurants and smiling at strangers. I didn't listen to a word of it. All I could think was my mother had killed Camellia and now Rosalie was gone too. But surely she'd just escaped town like she planned to. That had to be it. Rosalie was a free spirit, a wanderer and adventurer. Mother would never hurt her. She would never do that. She might hate what she represented, Father's infidelity, but she wouldn't hate Rosalie forever.

As I pushed the bicycle up the steps and locked it in place, I noticed I wasn't the only one running late for the bell. Students were gathered outside the front door, and a few teachers too. I heard people crying, and there was definitely a lot of whispering going on.

Despite my bloody knee and stained skirt, nobody paid a bit of attention to me until Janella Garner came racing toward me. Her face was twisted and her eyes were empty of tears, but she looked like she was doing her best to work up some.

"Isn't it horrible? She's dead! They found her dead, Bette! Right here in the playground! Naked on the merry-go-round." Janella grasped my arm, but I pulled away from her in horror. I didn't even have to guess who she was referring to. But she'd been gone for days and days. This couldn't be right. I had to hear for myself. I had to hear her say it.

"Who? Tell me." I said in a low, fierce voice. Janella took a step back as if she entirely regretted saying anything at all to me. "Who?" She wouldn't say, but it was clear that the entire school was being ushered out the front door. The chaos of it all threatened to overwhelm me, but the tumultuous crowd of gossips paid me no mind. Janella scrambled away and found someone else to share her fake tears with. But I could hear the whispers.

*Rosalie...gypsy girl...naked and murdered...who would do that?*

Finally, Miss Ferguson noticed me and squatted down in front of me.

"Bette, what happened to you?" She began to pat the bloody cut with her handkerchief.

"My bicycle. I fell off my bicycle, Miss Ferguson. Is it true? Is Rosalie really dead? I hear what people are saying. It can't be true. Can it?" A police car rolled up and quickly parked in front of the school. What was happening?

Miss Ferguson paused and would not look me in the eye. "I haven't seen her myself, Bette, but that's what the principal told the faculty. She is gone, Bette. I'm sorry to be the one to tell you such a thing. Were you friends? I didn't know her to have any friends."

"Yes, new friends." I wanted with all my heart to tell her the truth—that Rosalie was my sister—but another vehicle pulled up. A familiar black sedan.

Mother! Other cars pulled up too. Word of Rosalie's death had traveled quickly. Teens were fleeing to their parents, some of them weeping, all of them clearly upset.

Hypocrites! Most of them hadn't even known Rosalie or spoken to her at all. Now they wanted to cry at her death? I couldn't think. I couldn't reason. I didn't want to go with Mother. I didn't want to talk to her, see her, but she was honking the horn. What an inappropriate gesture! She couldn't even pretend to be sad about Rosalie's death.

"I better go. Thank you, Miss Ferguson." I grabbed my books and rose from the steps. I would have to leave my bicycle here. I could walk back and retrieve it later. Mother's incessant honking drove me mad. My heart was broken, totally broken, yet I could not cry. I wanted to cry like the rest of my schoolmates, people who didn't even know Rosalie. But I was her sister. I should go to her. I should go be with her. It was my right, wasn't it?

I stepped on the sidewalk steps clutching my books that I'd covered with brown paper bags. I rubbed the paper, but it did not comfort me. What to do? Should I run into the school and tell the police everything?

Tell them that my mother killed Camellia, confess to them that Rosalie was my sister?

I had a decision to make. It was now or never. Who would believe me, though? Sophisticated socialite Letitia Hollingsworth a murderer? I knew for a fact that she'd slaughtered Camellia like a lamb—I'd seen it all and felt Camellia's anger. She blamed me for her death.

As if Mother read my mind, she got out of her car and watched me from the sidewalk. Elegantly dressed in her business dress and heels, no one could have ever guessed that she was a murderess.

*I killed her for you, Bette. For you and me. She was a gnat that would not go away, even after all I've been through with her. I gave her money, begged her to leave, but she would not listen to reason.*

That had been the beginning of that horrible conversation. At some point I blacked out. Fainted at hearing Mother's confession. She murdered her in her own garden. Killed her with a garden tool. Left her to die, to bleed out on the ground like a bird shot from a tree. Left her like she was nothing, not a human being with a child of her own. I could hardly bear it.

I stood frozen on the sidewalk of my school. Waiting for what, I did not know.

Sensing my hesitation, Mother closed the car door and walked toward me, slowly but with purpose. More police cars arrived. The arriving police officials ran around her; she seemed not to notice. Nobody noticed. Sirens blared, teens were crying and arriving parents comforted them, but nobody saw Mother and me. They ran around us as we slowly walked to one another. It was a strange sensation, moving so slowly, being oblivious to everything and everyone else.

*Rosalie...it can't be true. You were supposed to leave with Byron. You were supposed to explore the world. What happened to you, Rosalie?*

Mother paused, and I took a step back. I didn't want to be here, but I could not leave the school without seeing for myself.

"Bette, come with me. Let's go." Mother glanced over her shoulder, clearly worried that others were approaching. What did she think I would do? Call her out? Maybe I would, but I had to see my sister.

"She's my sister," I whispered. "My sister." I took another step back as she paused on the grass. Would she come after me? Drag me to the car? No! I wasn't having it—I couldn't leave Rosalie alone. Not after what I knew. What I thought I knew. I turned and bumped into Miss Ferguson. She tried comforting me, but I pushed past her, and the next face and the one after that. It was much easier than I expected. Much easier to race down the long hallway. Nobody was in here. Nobody at all except a few teachers, and they were crying too. *Hypocrites, all of them! They had no idea what a beautiful soul she is—had been! Oh God! This can't be true!*

I made it to the outside doors at the end of the hallway, but I was blocked by a blue-clad police officer with bullish shoulders. "No, miss. You can't come out here. This is a crime scene. Leave the building, please."

"She's my...Rosalie! Oh God! It's her! It's really her!" Another cop covered Rosalie's body with a cloth. She hadn't been nude, but her dress had been torn and her feet were bare. "I have to see my friend!" I gasped and cried as I clutched at the wall of a man.

"You don't need to see her like this, young lady. Your friend wouldn't like that. Let's give her some privacy. Come on. It's alright. There, there." He escorted me out of the building and delivered me into the hands of my mother. She did not speak, and neither did I. Even when we left the school, even when we pulled into the drive of Hollingsworth Manor. Neither of us spoke.

By not saying anything, I was colluding with her. I needed to say something, didn't I? But what?

"I'll make us some breakfast, Bette. You left this morning without taking nary a bite. You need a good meal. It will do you good."

I couldn't believe she was suggesting that I eat and behave as if nothing had happened. As if Rosalie was some sort of cat that got hit by a car.

I walked into the house intending to ignore her, but I couldn't do it. "If you killed Rosalie, I'll know, Mother. She'll tell me."

"What are you talking about? She's dead. Keep your voice down. How dare you talk to me like that!" she growled back, but I didn't wait to argue with her. The grim-faced housekeeper met us and opened the door. She didn't speak to me, thankfully. I practically ran up the stairs and into my room. I collapsed on the bed and cried for what seemed like eternity. Nobody came to bother me. The utter despair, the grief, threatened to sicken me. It felt like a heavy blanket, one that would smother me.

Eventually I fell asleep. It was pitch black outside. I must have slept all day. I didn't have to wonder what to do next. I knew what I had to do. I changed my clothes; my knee hurt, but the wound had long stopped bleeding.

I put on a pair of blue jeans, a comfortable shirt and tennis shoes. My destination was clear. I had to go to Rosalie's house. I prayed that no one would be there. No police. Nobody. I knew what I had to do.

I had to talk to Rosalie!

Sneaking out of the house was not difficult. Mother was on the phone in the study talking to one of her snobby friends. Undoubtedly they would be nibbling over the details of Rosalie's death.

"It runs in that bloodline, I am told, Polly. Such wild creatures, those gypsies." Mother's condescending tone sickened me, but a small part of me tried to convince myself that she wouldn't do such a thing. Camellia? Yes, she'd been some sort of romantic rival, but Rosalie? An innocent girl?

I eased down the hall and slipped out the back door. It was chilly out, and I hadn't brought a jacket. I rubbed my arms and hurried into the woods. Now that I knew where Rosalie's house was, I had an idea. I would take a shortcut. If my guess was correct, the house would be about a half-mile away. The streets were busy, and lots of cars buzzed down Springhill Avenue. The walk was shorter than I expected, and I came upon Rosalie's house sooner than I anticipated. There were no lights on, but the door was closed. The pinwheels around the front garden fluttered in a low, lazy breeze.

"Rosalie?" I whispered into the darkness. Why? She was dead and couldn't hear me. My sister was gone, and I never got to tell her I loved her. I never got to see her children or share mine with her. We would not have the chance to do all the things sisters were supposed to do. I would never hear her voice again. "Sister," I said with tears in my eyes. Hovering around the woods, I glanced down the sandy pathway. Nobody came to challenge me or demand to know what I was doing. It was as if no one really cared that a beautiful girl was dead and gone. For what reason?

Running up the steps, I didn't bother knocking on the door. I reached for the handle, and to my surprise it opened. *No, I am not surprised. Rosalie wants me here.* I should never have left her that day, but I'd been so frightened. I was sure that Camellia would kill me. She wanted to kill me. Or hurt me.

The room was dark, but from what I could see nothing had been moved. The steamer trunk coffee table was in place. The couch was still carefully covered with a crocheted blanket. Even the tea set was right where we left it.

The cup of shadows!

I found a box of matches on the coffee table and struck one. Lighting the candle, I reassessed the room. I didn't want to turn on a lamp—that might draw too much attention, if anyone cared to look this way. Not that anyone would, but if Mother realized I was gone, she would certainly come here. Just in case she tried, I locked the door. And carrying the candle around, I checked all the windows. Everything was locked up tight. Her suitcase was still on the bed; Rosalie had been packed and ready to go. Why had Byron changed his mind? Maybe it was Byron who hurt her?

I went to the kitchen, but there was nothing to see except a plate of old food on the table. It must be days old. That didn't make sense. Her body had only been found this morning. So many questions, I had so many questions.

Could I do this? Could I see into the tea leaves with Rosalie's help? I had to look. I had to try. I heated the water on the stove and added the tea to the cup from Mother's tea set. I shuddered at the thought of using this cup to connect with my sister, but I had to. It was a lovely smell, one I would never forget.

A few minutes later, I set up the tray and carried it in the living room. I settled on the couch and began to cry. Why had I left her that day? I had been so afraid, so scared that Camellia would seek her revenge and harm me, but that wasn't what happened.

*Oh, God! She'd been trying to warn me, warn us! I'd failed to understand any of it. I'd run away. I would not do that again. If Rosalie was right—if I too had the ability to connect with the other side—I should be able to repeat the process. Could I do it?*

*I had to, for Rosalie!*

I poured the hot water in the cup, and the fragrance filled the room. I even lit the clove cigarette stub and took a few puffs in honor of Rosalie. Who knows? Maybe that was a part of the process? I had no idea, really.

After a minute of allowing the leaves to steep, I sipped the tea and left a swallow in the bottom. I swirled the cup as I'd seen Rosalie do. I had no idea what to look for. I could not interpret the symbols; I could not read them at all.

Hot tears slid down my face as I pleaded with Rosalie to help me. "I don't know what to do, sister. I don't know how to find you. I am so sorry. I know what Camellia meant, but I'm too late."

Nothing happened. No shadows. No voices. Nothing at all. The house was completely quiet. I cried softly as I put the cup down on the tray. I had to remember to take it home with me, sneak it back inside before Mother realized it was gone.

*What do I do now, Rosalie? Sisters forever. That's what you said. I am sorry, Rosalie.*

After a while, I began wandering around the house. The photos of Camellia and Rosalie broke my heart.

This had to be Rosalie's room. These were her beautiful things. Painted furniture, a worn quilt on her bed, a box on the nightstand. Why hadn't she packed that box? Sitting on the bed, I put the candle on the rickety table and opened it.

To my surprise, I found a picture of myself. It was from the school yearbook. She'd taken the time to cut it out and decorate it. In fact, she'd glued her picture next to mine and had written "Sisters" in silver ink beneath our pictures. I found other pictures of me, and Mother too. Just pictures. No letters or notes. Just pictures.

I wiped at my eyes and carried the box and candle to the front room. I put Rosalie's picture on the tray, propping it up so I could see us together. "Sisters forever," I whispered to my sister's lovely portrait.

I picked up the cup again and took another sip of the fragrant tea. That's when I heard a sound, a stirring beside me. I couldn't see anything, but I'd certainly heard it. I continued to stare into the murky depth of the teacup, and then it appeared.

The tiny ball of shadows returned, only this time I didn't run from it. "Rosalie...help me see. Please. I have to know what happened to you."

A face appeared, but it wasn't Rosalie's face. It was Byron's.

And Mother's! Oh, God! No!

The shadow grew and twisted, and then the color changed. It wasn't black anymore. It was as if I were watching a movie. A black and white movie. No, now it was color. I could see Rosalie's wide eyes; Byron strangled her, and the pain—I could feel it—it hurt so bad.

As I gasped for air, Byron strangled Rosalie, delivering one last kiss on her lips as she took her last breath. I screamed as she died, but then the scene changed.

Byron wasn't alone. Mother swung her car keys in her hand. "Quietly, Byron. Put her in the trunk." He grunted in answer and lifted Rosalie's body effortlessly. I watched in horror as he tossed Rosalie's body in the trunk of Mother's sedan. Her shoes hit the ground. Mother picked them up and tossed them in the trunk too, like they were just more rubbish. Like Rosalie had been rubbish too. Yes, I could hear her thoughts.

*She was trash and met her expected end. Only a few more loose ends.*

They sat in the car together, Byron in the passenger seat, Mother behind the wheel. They left Rosalie's house behind and took her body to an old barn. But Rosalie watched it all. She stayed near her body. She wasn't ready to leave yet. They would move her body again, once more. They would dump her on the playground because they couldn't agree on what to do with her.

*Rosalie...* I whispered as I watched the two of them argue. Mother paused and said, "Did you hear that?"

"No, I don't hear anything. Don't try to cheat me, Mrs. Hollingsworth. We had an arrangement."

I watched from the back seat. She handed Byron an envelope, obviously money, a pack of money. She paid him for his crime!

"This is nice, but don't forget my bonus. You promised me if I did it quickly you'd give me a bonus," he said as he smiled wickedly at Mother. I couldn't say what made me sicker, his smile or hers.

"Oh, I haven't forgotten, dear Byron. I never forget a thing. Trust me, I don't." And then she kissed him. I wanted to throw up, but I was trapped in the cup of shadows and I wouldn't run away. Not this time.

I could hear Mother's thoughts. She was going to kill him too. Not now. But soon. As soon as it was safe. He would be dead.

*Rosalie...I am sorry. I am so sorry...*

\*\*\*

Bette wept, and so did I. The cup of shadows vanished, and I was in the present. That was in the past. All of it.

Suddenly, Carrie Jo was there. I couldn't see her, but I felt her hand in mine. We were walking through the doorway of the Blue Room. As I stepped over the threshold, the honey hue of that strange dream world faded. I held on to her and cried, cried for Bette and Rosalie. Cried because I'd helped Bette deliver her message. She wanted someone to know that Rosalie was her sister. That her mother had been a murderess. In life, she didn't have the courage to stand up to her, to tell the truth.

But from beyond, she'd found a way. Now Bette would be at rest. Suddenly, Detra Ann was there and the three of us were crying and everything was going to be okay.

## *Epilogue—Aggie*

Dusting was my least favorite thing to do in the shop. It was a never-ending pain in the butt. There was just too much stuff that collected the infuriating annoyance. At least it was quiet. I didn't feel like dealing with window-shoppers today.

The bell chimed on the front door.

"Just when I thought I had escaped the looky-loos," I huffed under my breath, setting my dust rag down.

"Hello?" a male voice called out.

"I'm coming."

Running the shop by myself was something I had gotten used to since moving into the upstairs apartment. I was always there, and it just made sense for me to open and close up. I didn't mind, really, and appreciated that I could get the extra hours even around my school schedule.

The sound of a whole display falling sent me running toward the front. "What in the world? What happened in here? You'll have to pay for..."

Before I could get the words out of my mouth, I froze.

I couldn't believe it was *him*. Phoenix Mason. All the girls had a crush on him in high school. He was your typical bad-boy type. He had a real "rebel without a cause" vibe. I never took much interest because I knew he was way out of my league. Patrice could

*A Cup of Shadows*

have dated him—she was pretty enough. Smart enough. But he never even noticed me.

"I'm sorry. I knocked this over trying to look at the radio on the shelf," he said through his perfect rose-colored lips, handing me a pile of books. "I don't think I actually broke anything."

Gosh, he was gorgeous.

"It's okay, stuff like that happens all the time. There's too much stuff on the shelf, really. It's not your fault," I rambled on like a high school freshman.

"Do I know you?" he asked, showing his perfect white teeth. I swear this guy could be a model.

"Maybe," I stuttered. *Of course he's seen you, idiot. You went to the same school together since kindergarten. Geez. Get a grip, Aggie.*

"Yeah, I do know you. We went to school together, right?"

Maybe I wasn't invisible?

"Yes, I think so. Phoenix, right?" I replied, biting my lower lip. It was like a nervous twitch. I hated doing it, but I couldn't help it.

He pushed his shoulder-length brown hair back away from his face. "Yeah, you're Patrice's little sister."

*There it is. I'm always "Patrice the Perfect's baby sister."* Well, it wasn't her fault. I was a moth. A dull brown moth with a vivid red lipstick collection.

"Yep, that's me. I do have a name, though," I shot back unexpectedly.

"How is Patrice? I haven't seen her in a year or so, I guess," Phoenix said, rubbing his hand across the stubble on his chin. "Oh and sorry, I'm not so great with names. What was yours again?"

It never fails when it comes to guys. They see my sister and instantly fall head over heels for her, and I'm just the weird little sidekick. I swear sometimes I wish we could switch places, just for a day so I could see how it was to be Perfect Patrice. If they only knew that she was a weirdo like me. Just the thought of her cheerleader friends finding out that she had abilities made me laugh to myself.

"That makes sense. You remember Patrice's name and not mine. I get it. Are you looking to purchase anything today or just looking to break stuff?" I was losing patience with this bozo. His hotness was fading quickly the more he spoke.

"You're a feisty one," he said with a chuckle. "I actually wanted to buy the radio. Not break it."

One hotness point back—but only one. "Good. I need to sell something today. Come with me."

"Are you going to tell me or leave me in suspense?" Phoenix asked, leaning his elbow on the counter.

"How do you want to pay for this? It doesn't look broken. Should I plug it in to make sure?"

"No, it's fine." He pulled his wallet out of his back pocket and dug through it. "You really aren't going to tell me?"

"Tell you what?" I rang up the radio and slid his card through the machine.

"Your name."

The words fell out of his mouth like smooth butter. He actually wanted to know my name? I could have stared into those dark brown eyes forever. *Snap out of it, Aggie!*

"Mary Agnes, but most people call me Aggie."

"Okay, Aggie it is. Now can you wrap up the radio for me?"

"Of course," I replied, grabbing our best paper. I reached for the radio as Phoenix tapped on his cell phone. Probably texting his girlfriend. You couldn't trust hot guys like that.

Suddenly, static filled the air and the room appeared smoky. There was a jolt of electricity that flowed through my body like a shock wave.

A young lady with beautifully coiffed blond hair sat at her kitchen table weeping. She was dressed in what looked like 1940s attire. The radio sat on the counter. It was the radio from the shop. I tried to pick up the details of the room, but it was too smoky to make out any features. Whatever was playing on the radio sounded muffled. The whole vision looked strange, kind of shaky, like I was underwater.

There was a sweet floral scent that filled the air. Soft and unmistakable, the smell of gardenias. It was one of my favorite scents.

"Aggie?"

Phoenix's voice brought me back to the present. I was looking up at him from the floor.

"Are you okay? You passed out." He leaned over me, concern written all over his handsome face. Then he was helping me up.

My cheeks began to feel like I had a slight sunburn; I dusted myself off to distract from my embarrassment.

*Great Aggie, only you would pass out in front of one of your high school crushes.*

"I'm okay," I mumbled, "must be my iron or something." I couldn't believe I passed out. That was a first.

Phoenix gave me the side-eye as he let go of my arm. It was a look I'd seen many times before. The "okay, weirdo" look. Ugh.

He took the half-wrapped radio off the counter. "Are you sure you're okay?" he asked.

"Positive. No need to worry about me. Probably just need to eat something," I replied through a forced chuckle.

I wanted him out of the shop. I'd had enough embarrassment for the day.

"Okay, well, as long as you're sure you're okay. It was nice seeing you, Aggie."

"See ya later," I called out as he shut the shop door. Yeah, that was wishful thinking. Why would he ever come back here after that fiasco?

The scent of gardenias floated through the air past me, and the memory of the sobbing lady's face from my vision brought tears to my eyes. I could feel her sadness and longing. Longing for someone. The radio must have been hers at one time.

It made me wonder what her story was and why she was so sad. It was happening all over again. I guess this was something I just had to get used to working in an antiques shop.

So many connections and stories of the past were here waiting to be uncovered. Secrets that needed to be revealed. The one question played over and over in my mind, and I just couldn't let it go.

My intuition told me I'd see Phoenix again. That radio was what I called a "haunted thing." An active item.

The radio—or rather, the blonde—knew I was here. The radio would find its way back. It was going to make sure it came back to me.

And when it did, I would be ready.

## From A.E. Chewning

Where do I begin?

I guess the beginning is the best way to jump into this section, so let's start there.

M.L. Bullock graciously agreed to be my mentor at a time in my journey of becoming an author when I was, for lack of a better word, stuck in my endeavors. Her words of inspiration gave me the freedom to get back to writing and not let fear stop me from following my path into the world of ghost fiction and the paranormal.

With that being said, you can only imagine the pure joy I felt when I was asked to co-author this book with M.L. Bullock. It was truly a dream come true, and I was honored to join her in this endeavor. Especially when I found out that one of my favorite characters from the Seven Sisters series, Bette, would be featured and that part of her family history and mysteries would be revealed.

Mrs. Bullock gave me the task of developing a new character for the first book of her spin-off series, Devecheaux Antiques and Haunted Things. I jumped, or should I say dove, right in, and who came through to me was the character of Mary Agnes Kelly, or as she likes to be called, Aggie.

Aggie Kelly is a young college-aged girl who happens to have abilities. Like most people with abilities, she doesn't exactly know how to handle them or reveal them to her family...or anyone else, for that matter.

She is somewhat of an oddball, but she has come to terms with it and doesn't really mind being a little different. Truth be told, I think she enjoys being outside of the box.

Like most of the characters that I develop, Aggie is somewhat autobiographical. I connected to her in many ways and saw a lot of me in her little quirks, eccentricities and oddness. I was the band geek in high school who hung out with skaters, headbangers, musicians and artsy people. You would have definitely found me in t-shirts and blue jeans most days. Aggie's Van shoes are a nod to my beautiful daughter, Faith. She has her own fabulous sense of style and always amazes me how she can throw together anything and make it look great.

I look forward to writing more with M.L., exploring this world of the Devecheauxs and their haunted objects with Aggie, her family and her newfound friends.

The world of Devecheaux Antiques and Haunted Things is opening up, the haunted objects within have been released, and I'm happy to be a part of the exploration into this paranormal realm.

Happy reading,

A.E. Chewning

## *From M.L. Bullock*

Writing is by nature a singular activity. It can be a lonely road writing a short story or novel; not that I don't enjoy every minute of it, but it is lonely at times. About six months ago, another author reached out to me. She was experiencing a similar kind of loneliness. After we got to talking for a while, we both realized that we wrote in similar genres and enjoyed similar hobbies. You know how you meet someone and they immediately become a friend? That's what happened when I met Ashley Chewning.

Co-writing a book has been on my bucket list, but certain setbacks in my life made that impossible for a while. But when Ashley and I began "hanging out," I knew she was the author I wanted to write with. Thankfully, she said sure!

My biggest fear about bringing another author into my Seven Sisters world was that he or she would not be familiar with the story. That they would not appreciate the ins and outs of my paranormal world. With Ashley, that was not a concern because she knew the Seven Sisters books inside and out. I was delighted to offer her the co-author position for the Devecheaux Antiques and Haunted Things Book One, *A Cup of Shadows*.

I imagine if she knew that I would have a heart attack in the midst of writing this book—and that it would take months to finish—she might have said no, but maybe not. Ashley has a lot of moxie, and I like that about her.

I remember what it was like to write that first book way back in 2015. Eighty books later, I can honestly say that the hardest part of writing truly is the loneliness. Having someone on my team helping me bring my vision to life has been amazing. It has been an amazing experience. Ashley and I plan to write two more books in this series. I'm not sure what or how long this series will become, but for now we are just enjoying writing book by book.

Toward the end of the Seven Sisters saga, you may have noticed that I backed off a little on the characters of Detra Ann and Henri. It wasn't because I didn't love them or appreciate them; it was because I wanted to bring this series to you. There are so many things about this interesting couple that we don't yet know. I felt that they deserved their own series without Carrie Jo as the main star. Invariably, this story took me back to Carrie Jo, but only because she needed this moment with Bette to complete her own life. I think with this book we have been able to put all of the ghosts to bed from that original series. The series order for this world is Seven Sisters, Idlewood, Return to Seven Sisters, Gracefield and now Devecheaux Antiques and Haunted Things.

I like the idea of exploring the interesting topic of haunted items. What better place to do that than in an antiques store run by interesting characters that we want to know more about? At least I hope you want to know more about them.

Without you, this new series won't stand a chance. So, if you read it and enjoyed it, please leave a kind review. Recommend the book to a friend and share the cover. I love it, don't you?

I hope you were well entertained and that you will remember Detra Ann and Henri and Aggie long after you close the covers of this book. Drop me a line and let me know what you think about the new series.

You can reach me at authormlbullock@gmail.com or follow me on Facebook @AuthorMLBullock. I also have a newsletter, which I send out sporadically, usually about things I'm doing or research I'm conducting. It's not a consistent newsletter, but I do send out notes when I feel like there's something important to share with you. So if you're interested in staying connected, please add your name to the list at my website, www.mlbullock.com. I don't share my list with anyone, so no worries there.

Thanks again for reading. Thanks for stepping back into the shadows of Mobile, Alabama.

Until we meet again,

M.L. Bullock